In the
Shadow of Suribachi

by
Joyce Faulkner

Red Engine Press
Key West, FL

"The Menagerie" and "The Brafferton" first published in
Losing Patience, 2004 by Red Engine Press.

Library of Congress Control Number: 2005903038

ISBN – 10: 0-9745652-0-2
ISBN – 13: 978-0-9745652-0-2

Cover design and illustrations by Dianna C. Faulkner

Edited by Beth Lieberman

Printed in the United States of America

Quantity discounts are available on bulk purchases of this book for
educational institutions or social organizations. For information,
please contact the publisher:
Red Engine Press
1107 Key Plaza #158
Key West, FL 33040

To

Pvt. Billy Lee Plummer, USMC

And

All the other ghosts of Iwo Jima

Acknowledgments

A book like this takes years to compile. I humbly rely on the memory of those who chose to openly tell me their stories like Rusty Schneider, James Ashworth and other Marines who prefer to keep their identity private. Thanks to Ted Yund who put together a video tape of the battle from the movies taken by military photographers and stored in the National Archives. His work made it easier to describe many of the events in this book. I salute the authors of the books listed in the bibliography. Without your work, I'd never have been able to understand my father's stories and those of the other veterans.

The Brafferton is a beautiful old Inn in the heart of Gettysburg where we have stayed many times. I want to thank Maggie Abbott and Bill Ward for telling me how the history of their home related to the Battle of Gettysburg. They inspired me to write 'The Brafferton' as did Rusty Schneider. When you stay there, ask for 'The Battle Room'. The Minié ball is still in the mantle.

I also want to thank the historian in the Key West Public Library who spent hours one afternoon digging out yellowing newspaper articles describing the 1935 Labor Day hurricane in Islamorada. Even though I didn't catch his name, he is responsible for much of the detail included in 'Finding Paulina'.

Beth Lieberman is my editor and my rock. Without her encouragement and intelligent challenges my work would not be the growing, living thing that it is.

I also want to thank those folks who put up with my ponderings on a daily basis. Helen Jones is an intellectual and a terrific sparring partner. She always comes up with another side to consider. Mindy Phillips Lawrence is a good friend, fellow writer and editor with a sharp eye for details. What would I do without you, girlfriend? Dale Seawright, the cowboy poet, knows guns and is willing to share that knowledge. He's also good for a laugh any day of the week. Bobby Blades keeps me chuckling too. Beverly Walton-Porter is an enormous resource. Our many discussions on life in general and writing in particular keep me moving forward. Jim Radzinski was the first one to read *In the Shadow of Suribachi*. I appreciate his ideas, astute comments and encouragement. Ken Goldberg is always there with his quick wit and psychological insight -- and when he's NOT there I chase him down and make him answer my questions. Then there is that other great and twisted mind -- Ron Rakowski -- who agreed to take time to critique this work.

Finally, thanks to my family -- to my daughter Carmel Faulkner who is a critical part of every book I write, my son Nate Faulkner who can identify bullshit at twenty paces and does so with alacrity and to my cousin Karen Scott who drags me away from the computer once a week for Scottish Country Dancing. Most especially, to my husband John who hangs in there long after most folks would have thrown in the towel. Now more than ever, babe.

Foreword

I have known author, Joyce Faulkner, for only a short time. We became instant friends. Several common bonds link us -- one of the strongest being the love of great lessons in little stories.

Unlike Joyce, I was not raised on World War II stories at the knee of my father. No great warriors stand in the last century of my genealogy. However, I live in a place that concentrates on other battles from another time. By conscious effort or osmosis, we are all students of history. It prompts and pushes us every day. It's easy to see the difference between right and wrong in the passion of the moment. However, the passage of time shows that great events are fraught with compromise. History makes villains of some, heroes of others, and leaves many cloaked in veils of obscurity to protect the innocent and move society forward.

Two world wars and a deep economic depression marked the first half of the Twentieth Century. The people who lived through those traumas influenced the direction of today's society -- especially the soldiers and sailors and marines and airmen who participated in World War II. Unfortunately, the significance of the five war years is often lost on current generations. The experiences of these special men should rivet us, teach us and inspire us.

Some may express the truths of these stories in patriotism with flags unfurled and saluted -- a pledge of devotion upon their lips. Others may opt for the more quiet, but just as determined, approach of "paying forward" the dedication to improving humanity's lot begun by these men who were once so young. Regrettably, there will always be those who will allow the power shared herein to slip away from them, holding on to apathy and/or anger as buoys through the seas of suffering.

Whatever path one takes, it is the writer who marks the page for posterity, bringing to life ghosts that have haunted, and will yet haunt, others who walk similar fields of battle. Difficult times demand difficult measures, initiating battles within. Though not obvious, these silent struggles are often the hardest and most painful. In this light, Joyce joins an honorable multitude who wield their pens believing that little stories tell of momentous moral struggles and impact the path of our lives.

The "Great Generation" is slowly leaving us. Their stories, told with passion and long overdue compassion, should draw us to them and remind us that life is to be lived in all its aching glory. Rare voices say it with as soft a touch, yet as penetrating a needle as this.

Maggie Abbott, Gettysburg, PA

Introduction

In a way, I began writing this book when I was a child and my father suffered a nervous breakdown. Twelve years after the Battle of Iwo Jima, the stress of those thirty-six days haunted his days and nights. He couldn't eat or sleep and he couldn't articulate exactly what it was that was bothering him. It surfaced in drugged snippets told out of context. I had no idea what he meant most of the time -- I just knew it was something bad. He was proud to be a part of the great effort of his generation and happy to have survived when so many others didn't. Yet he saw and did things that broke his heart and he grieved for friends lost forever. It wasn't until long after he died when I began the research that supports this work that the pieces of the puzzle came together. I don't begin to understand what it was like. I'm a writer and these are stories. What happened on that sulfuric-smelling island in February and March of 1945 is indescribable. Maybe that's why so many of those who lived it have chosen not to try.

Joyce Faulkner, April, 2005

In the Shadow of Suribachi

Finding Paulina...1
Brothers and Arms.. 15
Colored Stones.. 30
The Menagerie..42
Sweet Tooth Tommy... 55
Kendall's Dream Girl..71
Cordell's Luck.. 84
Iwo Jima... 99
    Chapter 1 -- At Sea.. 100
    Chapter 2 -- The Night Before.................................104
    Chapter 3 -- The Prelude... 112
    Chapter 4 -- The Beach...128
    Chapter 5 -- The First Night.....................................134
    Chapter 6 -- The Second Day................................... 140
    Chapter 7 -- The Long Haul..................................... 142
    Chapter 8 -- Smitty.. 148
    Chapter 9 -- Kirby..156
    Chapter 10 -- The Last Day...................................... 161
A Grateful Nation..165
The Brafferton.. 186
Historical Notes.. 198
Bibliography...206

Finding Paulina

Islamorada, Florida -- 1935

It had been two days since the hurricane hit. The Keys were awash with garbage and corpses. Paradise turned into hell overnight. Emil Kroner stared at the scene in front of him with his mouth agape. "Here!" It came out a hoarse whisper. He turned and waved. "HERE!"

"Coming!" One of the other searchers called.

"HURRY! HE'S ALIVE!"

Emil waded through the sandy water and lifted a piece of corrugated tin away from the injured man. At some point, borne on the wind, it had been lethal -- but fortuitously wedged between the tree and a rock, it became an instrument of salvation -- acting first as a barrier from other flying objects and then as shelter from the unfriendly elements.

The man had tied himself to the battered palm tree with a belt and a twisted bed sheet. He had a large gash on his forehead that had long since stopped bleeding and crusted over. His limbs hung at impossible angles like those of a broken puppet. Emil cringed at the sight of bones pressing through what was left of the heavy trousers, but the face was far worse. Wind, sand and water had blasted skin and hair from the head and upper torso rendering the victim unrecognizable.

"Mister?"

No answer.

Emil reached out to brush away the flies congregating on the man's body.

"Leave me alone," the man groaned.

Emil jerked back his hand. "Are you okay?" It was an inane thing to say to a man with no face.

"Leave me to die in peace."

"I NEED HELP OVER HERE," Emil screamed over his shoulder.

"It'll be a while. Do what you can." The rescuers had found a small child lying on a desk floating a few yards from shore. Bloated and fish-belly white, it looked dead to Emil, but they had to try even if the chances were a hundred to one, they had to try.

He turned back to the man lashed to the tree. Unable to loosen the wind-tightened knots on his bindings, he must have been dangling there for almost thirty hours. Emil couldn't imagine such agony. "Let me make you more comfortable," he said.

The man sucked air through his broken teeth and nodded.

"I'm Emil. What's your name?" Emil stripped off his shirt and wrapped it around the man's shoulders.

"Andreas Dion." The voice was raspy as though he had a throat full of sand too.

"I'm gonna cut you down now, Andreas."

"I can't see."

"I know." What the sand had done to Andreas's eyes made Emil feel sick. "I'm going to put my arm around you to keep you from falling when I cut you loose. Try to help me if you can." It was a stupid thing to say. Andreas was as limp as a rag doll.

2

"Do what you have to do."

Emil sawed through the sheets with a pocketknife. It took a long time but he freed Andreas and pulled him away from the water lapping at the foot of the tree. Andreas's screams were guttural wheezes. It took everything Emil had to drag him to a dry spot on the beach.

"There," Emil said as rolled up his undershirt and stuffed it under the injured man's head. "We'll wait here until the others can help me get you to Mackenzie's place. They've set up a hospital in that movie theater he's building."

Andreas struggled to breathe. "Tell them not to bother. I won't last long."

Distracted, Emil watched his comrades fish the baby's body out of the ocean. It looked like Louisa Sherman's little girl what with all that black hair. Last he heard there was no word as to what had happened to Louisa herself.

"I need you to find my wife." Andreas tried to lift his head. "Her name is Paulina."

"Is she from around here?" Emil had lived in the Keys all his life. He'd never heard of anyone named Paulina.

"Times are bad. I got a job working on the overseas highway. I've been living in the camp and she was with her uncle in the panhandle. It took me months to put together enough money so she could come see me. She got here last week."

There were hundreds of bodies strewn over the narrow islands and floating in the surf. Paulina was probably one of them, but Emil didn't want to tell Andreas that. "You were in the war?" Many of the highway workers were veterans hit hard by the depression.

Andreas grunted.

3

A few yards away, someone whistled. Emil shook his head and shrugged. The rescuer nodded and went back to searching the shoreline for more victims. It didn't take a doctor to know that Andreas was dying. There wasn't much Emil could do and there were so many more out there. He ought to move on too.

"You can't fix me," Andreas said as though he were reading Emil's mind.

"You're going to be fine."

"Look, son. I got a lung full of sand. Even if my innards weren't beaten to mush by that wind, I'd still die of pneumonia before nightfall." The man paused as though the effort to expel that many words exhausted him.

Emil squatted beside Andreas's battered body, not wanting to stay and watch him suffer but unable to walk away.

"I can hear you breathing."

"I got nothing better to do." Emil wiped his eyes with the back of his hand, glad that the man couldn't see his tears. "Maybe I'll just keep you company for awhile."

Andreas relaxed back into the sand. "You damn fool."

"Tell me about Paulina," Emil said to avoid thinking about Andreas's predicament. "Where should I look for her?"

Andreas struggled to breathe. "They were -- evacuating us. Everyone was trying to get -- on the train but I had to -- find Paulina. She was staying with the Griffins -- down the beach. They were -- all gone -- when I got there. The place was a mess -- doors wide open, sheets cut up and laying everywhere. I grabbed one -- just in case -- and struck out -- to look for them."

Emil closed his eyes. The Griffin house was gone, blown away. They'd found Hank's body not far from the road impaled by a fence post. Someone told him that Evangeline and one of the kids had disappeared under the huge tidal wave

4

that swept over the island. Who knew what happened to the other two? Last he heard, Jack was the only Griffin to survive and the old man was in pretty bad shape, unable to tell anyone about Paulina. "Maybe they already found her. I'll check at the hospital."

Andreas shivered. "Never met -- anyone like her."

"A pretty one, eh?"

"Inno--." Andreas's voice faded.

"What?" Emil leaned forward.

"Innocent -- no past to burden her, no future -- always now."

"I'm sorry?"

"After Belleau Wood, I was -- shattered -- but Paulina is a force of nature -- like fresh air and green grass. She helped me -- start over."

Andreas made no sense. Grief and pain, Emil figured. "You were a soldier?"

"5th Marines."

"You must be proud. I'm going to enlist when I finish high school."

"Argh." It was a wet gurgle.

Emil waited for Andreas's coughing spasm to subside. "I thought you'd understand."

"Yes."

"My mother doesn't. It's the first time I've wanted to do something that she hasn't backed me."

"Mothers -- don't raise -- their sons -- to be Marines."

Emil couldn't tell if the edge in Andreas's voice was pain or bitterness. "Can't be a momma's boy all my life. Besides, if she loved me she'd want this for me."

"My mother -- begged me -- not to go."

"But you did anyway. Right?"

"I was -- eighteen." Andreas ran his tongue over his torn lips. "There was -- a war."

"That's just it. There isn't any war right now. I don't know what she's so worried about."

Andreas's body quivered as though he was fighting some immense battle in his mind, or maybe he was crying. It was hard to tell. "Fingers -- and toes."

"What?"

"When you were born -- your mother counted your fingers --." Andreas didn't have enough air to finish the sentence.

Emil glanced at his own hands. "That sounds like my mom all right."

"Listen -- to her."

"But I love my country. Whenever they play the Stars Spangled Banner I get goose bumps. When I think of all the men who died so that I could be free, I want to be like them. Like you."

Andreas shook his head. "Not -- like me."

"I want my life to have mattered. I'm a kid from a poor family. I'll be a fisherman like my dad. It's not an easy life, you know. Day after day of backbreaking work. I want more. I want to be remembered because I did something important."

"There are -- other ways -- better ways."

"It's about being a part of something bigger, about being part of a team." It seemed like the perfect way to live to Emil.

"Find -- Paulina."

Emil glanced down at Andreas wondering what Paulina had to do with being a Marine. The man arched his back, clenching his jaws. He'd been selfish, Emil realized, blabbing on about what HE wanted while this poor soul was dying. "Hey fella, I'm sorry."

Andreas writhed as he struggled to take in his last breath. Emil forced himself to touch the raw cheek and watched Andreas die. He was still squatted beside the body when his father found him an hour later.

"Are you okay, boy?" Max Kroner put his hand on Emil's shoulder.

"It stinks out here."

"Breathe through your mouth."

"Doesn't help."

"They told me what you did. He was a big man. Couldn't have been easy getting him over here."

"No."

"You did good."

Emil hung his head. He'd been a fool, yammering on about the Marines and not getting the information that he needed before Andreas died. "He wanted me to find his wife."

"I'm afraid that might be impossible."

"I gotta try. Even if the odds are against her. I owe him that much."

Max nodded. "Let's go try then."

Emil chewed his lip not wanting to leave the faceless corpse alone on the beach.

"He ain't going to wash away where you got him," Max said finally. "We're hunting for live ones now."

Emil nodded and they stood up.

"He was a Marine."

Max took a deep breath.

Emil knew his father was tired of being the referee between Emil and his mother. Besides this was no time to worry such a sore topic. "He came looking for Paulina rather than catching the train."

They stared at each other.

"Oh my God," Max said. "Maybe she went looking for him there."

The storm had washed the train off the tracks. The cars crushed many of those already aboard. Flying debris killed others and the tidal wave swept the rest into the ocean. If Paulina had gone looking for Andreas at the train station, it wasn't likely that they'd find her alive.

"I don't even know what to look for," Emil said.

"No idea what she looks like?"

"He didn't say."

Max Kroner put his arm around Emil. "We might try Mackenzie's place. Maybe Jack Griffin is awake by now."

• • • • •

Filled with injured people and folks trying to help them, the partially completed concrete structure was one of the few buildings to withstand the fury of the Labor Day storm. Jack Griffin lay on a cot just inside the door. Beneath a bloodstained bandage covering his forehead, his nose was broken and both eyes were black.

Emil touched his foot. "Jack?"

The old man's eyes glittered through swollen slits. "Emil. Max."

"How are you doing?" Max Kroner took off his hat.

Jack licked his lips. "Powerful thirsty."

"You hang in there and I'll find you something."

Emil knelt beside the cot while Max went looking for water. "They say you're going to be okay. Cuts and bruises and a concussion."

The old man sighed. "Not much left out there, is there?"

Emil shook his head.

"I've got a niece in Galveston."

"Good."

"Your family came out okay?"

"It wasn't so bad down our way." The Kroners had crouched in their 'hurricane house' for hours. It wasn't until the storm died down and they emerged from the shelter that they saw that the devastation was far worse than anyone remembered ever seeing before.

"Here ya go, buddy." Max Kroner slipped an arm under Jack's head and held a cup of water to his parched lips.

"Thank you." Red streaked the whites of Jack's eyes. "They gave me something so I'll sleep."

Emil was afraid Jack might not wake up for awhile. "I gotta ask you something before we go."

"What?" Jack's voice was becoming dreamy.

"What happened to Paulina?"

Jack's lucidity returned. "Paulina?"

9

"Your house guest."

"OH GOD! I forgot Paulina." Jack tried to sit up, put both hands to his bandaged head and dropped back onto the cot. "You have to go get her."

"Where is she?"

"Most extraordinary woman I ever met. She makes a man feel that miracles are possible."

"Is she alive?"

He winced as if in pain. "When it started, I took her over to the Mitchell's well house and locked her in."

"Why did you do that?"

"The world is a dangerous place for Paulina. Someone has to take care of her. I couldn't leave her to wander alone in the storm while I tended to Hank and Evangeline and the kids."

"Mitchell's well house is made out of cement blocks," Max whispered. "She might be okay."

"It was the most incredible thing." The old man rolled his head from side to side, his eyes fluttering. "The hurricane was upon us as we ran toward Mitchell's house. Paulina giggled and twirled around with her arms open. She was like an angel in the night, her hair swirling in the wind, not afraid of anything. Then right over her head lights started flashing and crackling, like lightning but it wasn't. It was magic."

"Probably static electricity. Lot of sand in the air," Max said behind his hand to Emil.

"As scared as I was, I was at peace." Jack let his arms drop onto the cot beside his body. "God blesses Paulina's protectors and I was blessed to be one."

Emil glanced at his father who shrugged. Was the old man nuts?

10

"So you locked her in the well house," Emil urged Jack who was beginning to drift away. "What happened then?"

"I came back for my family but the house was gone, blown away into the night. My daughter-in-law and grandchildren were gone too. I staggered toward the road fighting the wind. I found my son but he was dead, skewered by that post."

"I'm sorry, Jack." Max patted the old man's hand.

"Don't you see? The worst was while I was struggling with the lock, protected by the well house. I'm alive because of Paulina."

The old man's grief was hard to watch. Emil glanced at his father, strong and fit and well. After so much devastation, it didn't make sense that no one in the Kroner family had been hurt. He said a quiet prayer of thanksgiving. He figured Max was doing the same.

"We need to let you get some rest." Emil pulled Jack's sheet up higher on his chest.

Jack grabbed his wrist. "Find her."

Emil recoiled in surprise. "I'll go get her now. I promise."

"Take care of her."

"Emil's just a boy, Jack. He can barely take care of himself." Max clapped Emil on the back. "But we'll make sure someone looks after her."

"It's you now."

Emil peeled the old man's fingers off his wrist. "Okay. Okay."

●●●●●

Emil rubbed his arm as he and Max headed out to the Mitchell place. "What happened to him?"

11

"Got hit by a shingle, they say. Right between the eyes."

"Did it make him crazy or was he always that way?"

Max sighed. "After what he's been through, it's not any wonder his mind is wandering."

"Makes you wonder what's so special about this Paulina, doesn't it? Andreas couldn't have been more than thirty-five and he was nuts about her. Jack's seventy if he's a day. They both talked about her like she was this saint or something."

"Times have been tough. Maybe both of them saw so much ugliness in this world that a pretty girl made them feel better, hopeful maybe."

"I like girls as much as the next guy, but I never saw one that was magic." In fact, Emil hadn't seen one that would make him want to change his plans about the Marines. Not that cute brunette in English class nor the little red head in Math.

"That just means you haven't met the right one yet."

"You mean Mom was magic?" Emil elbowed Max.

"You damn right she was. Still is. She makes my life worth living."

Emil blushed. "Aw, Dad." It was hard to think of his parents as lovers. Still it felt good somehow. "Here we are walking down a road with bodies lying in the ditches and we are talking like things were okay. What's wrong with us?"

"Reminding ourselves that after this is over, life will begin again."

"Yeah?"

"Yeah."

They turned into the Mitchell's front yard. There was no sign of Gene and his wife. The family's soggy belongings were scattered everywhere -- clothes tangled in the bushes, picture albums floating in puddles of seawater. Their old Ford had tumbled across the driveway and lay on its side in the ditch. The hurricane had destroyed both the house and garage. However, the walls of the well house at the far end of the property survived even though the roof had blown away.

Emil broke into a run. The door hung on one hinge. A small figure was inside. At first, he thought that she was dead, then he heard soft grunts. Her damp nightgown was pulled up over her thighs, her hands cupping her round belly. Her blond hair fell forward over her face as she pushed.

"Paulina?"

She ignored him until the contraction passed, then looked up at him. The sun broke through the clouds and illuminated her face. Her smile was joyous, her eyes as guileless as an animal's. Emil stepped forward. "Are you okay?"

She nodded.

"Can you talk?"

She shook her head.

"Can I help you?"

She shook her head. Another contraction began. Her cheeks turned red as she bore down to push the baby out.

"DAD!"

"I'm here, son."

"What do we do?"

"Let nature take its course."

Emil squatted down in front of her. "She's retarded I think. Or mute."

"Don't touch her with death on your hands," Max warned.

13

"Then what?"

"She'll do it by herself."

"Then what?" Emil repeated as he watched the small dark head emerge.

Paulina delivered the child, a red faced boy. She picked up the baby and poked her finger in his mouth. He howled. She turned him over examining his rump, his penis, the pulsing cord still connecting him to her. Touching the tiny fingers and toes, she looked up into Emil's eyes and smiled.

Brothers and Arms

Fort Smith, Arkansas –– 1937

Bill Zimmer hid in his mother's closet watching her through the half-closed door. She drew skinny half-moons over her eyes with a black eyebrow pencil and sat back to admire herself in the mirror.

Bill's brother RL stood in the doorway to her bedroom, arms folded over his chest. "You're going out again?"

"I am, if it's any of your beeswax, Mr. Nosey." She puckered her lips and painted them dark red. "You and Bill and Little Mack can go see Grandpa Sam at the dairy while I'm gone."

"We were there yesterday," RL said. "Grandpa Sam's busy bottling up this morning's milk. Bill and Little Mack get in the way."

Bill frowned and burrowed deeper into his hiding place. It was little Mack who got in the way. Not Bill.

"Don't be silly," Nita Zimmer replied. "Your dad was littler than Little Mack when he started playing in that dairy."

"But why can't we stay home? All our toys are here."

Nita used her finger to make little waves in her short hair. "You're a kid. It's not up to you to question an adult."

"Yes, ma'am."

She rummaged through her jewelry box. "Here." She held out her arm. "Come fasten this bracelet for me."

RL scowled. "Aw, Mama."

Bill knew RL hated fooling around with their mother's jewelry, but Bill would gladly fasten the bracelet -- only Nita never asked him.

"Come on, now." Nita shook her hand.

RL squinted, fussing with the tiny lock. "How long will you be gone?"

"I don't want to see you back here until a quarter to four. Not a minute sooner."

"Can we have lunch first?"

"Grandpa Sam will give you a cinnamon, sugar and butter sandwich."

"What will Dad say about this?"

Nita spun around and slapped RL, leaving her hand print on his cheek. "He won't say anything because he won't know anything."

Bill gasped. He'd never seen their mother hit RL before. He was her favorite. RL's face got red but he didn't flinch or touch his cheek. Bill knew that even though RL was hurt and mad, he'd never cry. That was the thing about RL. He never cried no matter what anyone did to him.

"Now, go get your brothers and get them ready to go down to Grandpa Sam's."

"Bill's hiding again."

"Then go find him." Nita squirted herself with the perfume the boys had bought her at the dime store. "Right now."

RL turned around and Bill could see he was still mad.

"And close the door behind you. I'm dressing."

RL slammed the door knocking over a glass angel that stood on Nita's dresser. It bounced off the iron bedstead and smashed into pieces.

"My angel," Nita wailed. "I can't believe you broke my angel." She knelt and gathered up the little bits of glass, tears running down her cheeks.

Bill couldn't stand to see his mother's grief. He slipped out of the closet and ran to her. "I'll help you p-pick it up, M-Mama."

"Stay away from me." Nita fended him off. "I don't have time for you now."

Bill backed into a corner, afraid she might hit him too.

"RL?" She tried to fit the pieces of the figurine back together. "Where are you? I need you."

RL opened the door with Little Mack in hand. "What's wrong?"

"You broke my angel." The way her chin quivered made Bill feel bad for her. "The one big Mack gave me the day we got married."

"I didn't mean to." RL looked sad too.

"You know how dear this is to me."

"I'm sorry, Mama. Maybe we can glue it back together."

She sniffed. "You think?" Bill marveled at how quickly she made up with RL. When she got mad at HIM, it seemed like she stayed mad a long time -- and she never got mad at Little Mack.

"Sure. I bet we can do it."

"Mama!" Little Mack held out his arms.

Nita gathered RL and Little Mack into her arms. "I don't

17

know what I'd do without you boys."

Bill stood in the corner by himself wondering if she meant him too.

• • • • •

"Bring home a chicken for supper, RL." Nita called as the boys traipsed down the front steps in single file.

"Okay, Mama."

The screen door slammed as Nita went back inside.

"I h-hate k-killing chickens." Bill grumbled as they reached the edge of the yard. "I c-can't stand l-looking at all that b-blood."

The screen door crashed open. "Have Grandpa Sam give you some butter."

"Okay, Mama."

Bill thought it was more fun to go through the field than to walk down the road. Little Mack did too. RL held up the barbed wire so Bill and Little Mack could squirm through.

"I wanna carry buttah!" Little Mack jumped up and down and clapped his hands while RL slithered under the fence after them.

"I'm g-gonna c-carry the b-butter, squirt." Bill elbowed Little Mack.

"OW!" Little Mack squealed and pushed him back.

"Will you two stop it?" RL stepped in between them.

"I d-don't w-want t-to c-carry a d-dead chicken." Bill stuck out his lower lip and clenched his fists.

"We'll have Grandpa wrap the butter up into two packages and you can both carry one, how's that?"

18

RL always took care of things like that. In fact, Bill counted on RL far more than he did their father who was always out of town and his mother who was always getting ready to leave to meet her friend. "Okay. But n-no chicken."

"I'll carry the chicken."

The boys heard the screen door slam one more time as RL led them across the field and into the woods.

Half way down Bailey Hill, Little Mack spied a blackberry bush and stopped to grab as many berries as he could and cram them into his mouth.

"He's stealing b-blackberries again," Bill called. "Uncle Jimmy's g-gonna b-be pissed."

RL turned around. "Come on, Mack. Grandpa Sam's waiting for us."

"I'm hungry." The berries stained the little boy's lips and tongue dark red.

"Grandpa Sam'll give us a sandwich."

"More." Little Mack stuffed handfuls into his pocket and still more into his mouth.

"I'm g-gonna t-tell on you." Bill stuck his thumbs in his ears and waved his hands. "Neener, neener, neener."

RL sighed and came back up the hill to fetch Little Mack. The little boy wiped his hands on his coveralls and stood up, his cheeks bulging with berries. "Comin'."

"Okay. Let's go." RL herded Bill and Little Mack past Uncle Jimmy and Aunt Sara's barn.

"Look at you guys." It was laundry day at Aunt Sara's. She was pinning towels onto the clothesline. "What have you been up to, Little Mack?"

"I'm sorry, Aunt Sara," RL said. "He'd already got into them before I caught him." The boys had been warned many times to stay away from those bushes but Little Mack always forgot. What a dunce Little Mack was, Bill thought.

Little Mack peered around RL's leg and grinned.

"You scamp. Stealing our blackberries again?" Aunt Sara wasn't really mad.

Bill frowned at his baby brother. If it was Bill with blackberry juice all over his face, it would be a different story. Why was no one ever mad at Little Mack?

"What are you guys doing down here again anyway? What's going on with Nita?"

RL put his hand over Little Mack's face. "She's got to go into town today."

"Something wrong?"

"Naw, every thing's fine."

"No trouble with your Dad up there in Michigan?"

"No. He's fine. Sends us a check every payday."

Little Mack giggled and popped out on the other side of RL's leg. RL tried not to grin and put his other hand over the boy's face.

"He's such a little angel!" Aunt Sara smiled at Little Mack. "How did he get that mop of curly blond hair when the rest of you are so dark?"

RL frowned and shrugged.

"It's a damn shame when a man has to leave home to get work."

"Yes, ma'am."

"This depression's tore up more than one family."

"It sure has." RL patted Little Mack on the head.

When people asked about Little Mack, it made Bill mad. The kid was a pain, but he was Bill's brother same as RL.

"Did you boys have lunch?"

"We're fine, ma'am. Grandpa Sam'll take care of us."

"Not right now he won't. He had to shoot a cow this morning. He and Jimmy took the carcass off to the butcher about an hour ago."

"Which c-cow?" Bill spent a lot of time in the dairy. Killing chickens for dinner made him queasy. He couldn't imagine shooting bigger animals like Flossy or Beulah.

"That little black and white heifer he got last May. I forget her name."

"Suzie?" Bill had been messing around in Suzie's stall just yesterday. She was a friendly little cow. Didn't mind at all when kids crawled around under her hooves.

"What happened to her?"

"She got out last night. Don't know how. Jimmy swears he closed and fastened the gate to her stall but somehow she must have worked it free. Once she was loose inside the barn, she nosed open that rickety old door and wandered down on Jenny Lind where a truck hit her."

Bill tried to remember if he closed the door to Suzie's stall after he got his ball back. He wasn't sure. He felt sick to his stomach. Was it his fault? Did poor Suzie die because of him?

"I'm sorry to hear it." RL shook his head. "She sure was a nice little heifer."

"Wasn't like she was a person or nothing, but it was sad to

see her hurting like that and of course, it puts your Grandpa back a mite financially. Anyway, there ain't anyone down in the barn right now. Why don't you boys come on in and I'll make you a sandwich?"

"Thanks, Aunt Sara. We'd sure appreciate it." RL pushed Little Mack forward and they trooped down to the farmhouse she shared with their Uncle Jimmy.

Bill followed at a distance. This was the worst thing he'd ever done. He hoped no one ever found out he'd been playing in her stall. Poor Suzie. Poor Grandpa Sam.

"And you know RL Zimmer that your mother expects you to keep a better eye on that young'n there. It's not the blackberries so much but what if he'd got hold of something that would make him sick?"

"What kinda sammich?" Little Mack tugged on Aunt Sara's skirt.

"How about grilled cheese?"

Little Mack nodded. "And milk?"

"All you want, sugar."

"I promise I'll watch him better." RL ran his hand through Little Mack's curls as they went inside.

Bill waited until they closed the door behind them before trotting down to the barn. It had all kinds of hiding places. He'd find a good one and think about things until he felt better or hungry or they found him. The doors were wide open. The other cows were out in the pasture. He tiptoed past the stalls pausing for a minute in front of Suzie's. She'd had big black eyes and a soft nose. He stuffed his hands in his pockets and kicked at the straw on the floor. "D-damn c-cow. I d-didn't l-like her anyway."

The ladder to the loft was at the back of the barn. He

climbed up one step at a time. It was scary being up so high, but exciting too. He hefted himself over the edge and stood up. The floor squeaked. A nail had worked loose a long time ago and Uncle Jimmy had never gotten around to fixing it.

Bill blinked. "Wow!" Grandpa Sam's shotgun lay propped against a bale of hay near the open window. Bill looked around. Aunt Sara and RL and Little Mack were still in the farmhouse. They hadn't even noticed he wasn't with them yet. Reaching for the gun, he stubbed his toe on the nail and fell on his stomach.

"D-damn." There was no one to hear him curse anyway.

Crawling over to the shotgun, he ran his hand along the long black barrels. "Wow," he repeated. It was almost as long as he was tall. Grandpa Sam would never let him play with it. In fact, this was the first time someone left it where he could see it up close. He touched the triggers with the tips of his fingers. The stock was so smooth. He tried to lift it to his shoulder but it was heavy and he nearly dropped it.

Laying the barrels over the bale, he squatted and pretended to shoot out the window. "Bam, bam!" He wondered if Grandpa Sam remembered where he left it? Maybe he could take it to his favorite hiding place in the woods and play with it there. Maybe no one would notice it was gone. Maybe Grandpa Sam would think it was lost until Bill was through looking at it. Yeah. That's what he'd do.

He dragged it across the loft until he got to the ladder. He stopped wondering how to get down with the big gun in tow. He thought about dropping it onto the floor of the barn but was afraid the fall might break it. He didn't want to make Grandpa Sam mad at him. After a bit, he turned around and started down the steps backwards. Two steps down, he tried to grab the gun by the barrel and pull if off the edge of the loft.

23

"Bill?" Little Mack peered around the edge of the barn doors. "You here?"

Bill knew if Little Mack saw the gun he'd tell RL and then RL would tell Aunt Sara and then Aunt Sara would take it away from him and tell Grandpa Sam or his mother.

"Little Mack? Did you find Bill?" It was RL's voice. He was only a few steps behind Little Mack.

Bill tried to push the gun back on the floor of the loft so Little Mack and RL wouldn't see it. The stock hit the protruding nail and he nearly fell backwards. Letting go of the barrel to grab the ladder railing, he saw the gun teeter over the edge for a moment and then drop to the barn floor. When it hit the ground, it went off. The blast was so loud that Bill scurried back up into the loft, screaming. The noise echoed throughout the barn. He held his hands over his ears and closed his eyes.

"LITTLE MACK!" RL shrieked.

Bill heard footsteps running away from the barn.

More yelling in the distance. "AUNT SARA!"

Bill peeked over the edge of the loft. Little Mack lay on the floor just inside the barn doors. The shotgun was close by. The kid was a mess. He must have gotten blackberry juice in his hair. Bill leaned over further. There was blackberry juice on his coveralls too. Lots of it.

Little Mack lay so still. What was wrong? The kid was always moving, even when he was asleep. Bill cocked his head. There was so much blackberry juice -- a pool of it. Then it hit him. BLOOD! Like the chickens out back, like Suzie. The shotgun blast must have hit Little Mack. NO! Bill scooted backwards across the floor of the loft and hid behind the hay bale, his hands over his face.

More screams in the barn below as RL returned with Aunt

24

Sara. "Oh you poor baby." There was rustling. Bill imagined Aunt Sara picking up that still little body. "RL, I don't care who Nita has up there, you go get your mother and get her down here."

"Yes ma'am." RL sounded scared.

More footsteps as RL ran out of the barn. Bill imagined him running up Bailey Hill, through the woods and the field, jumping over the barbed wire fence. He'd jerk open the screen door and go into the house yelling for their mother. She'd be in her bedroom, trying to glue the glass angel back together. Bill saw her face -- her eyes wide, her mouth a perfect 'O' as RL told her about Little Mack and the shotgun.

In the barn below, Aunt Sara's keening grew louder. "What did you do to yourself, baby? What did you do to yourself?"

Bill heard Grandpa Sam's truck coming up the driveway. It stopped and the door slammed. He heard Uncle Jimmy's voice -- and Grandpa Sam's as they came toward the barn.

"Get in here, Jimmy. There's been a horrible accident."

Aunt Sara's screams must have scared the men. Bill heard them running. The barn door popped open. "OH SHIT, NO!" That was Uncle Jimmy.

"Where the hell did this poor little guy find the shotgun?" That was Grandpa Sam. His voice was gruff. Bill had never heard his grandfather sound that way before. Suddenly, he realized Sam Zimmer was crying.

"Shit, shit, shit." Uncle Jimmy was breathless. "I must have left it in the loft after we took care of Suzie this morning. I never thought Nita'd send the kids back down today. What have I done?"

"Where's the other boys, Sara?"

"I haven't seen Bill. RL went to get Nita."

"Someone better call Big Mack."

Bill's thoughts turned to Little Mack. Where was he now? Was it like being asleep? Did it hurt him? He was a pain in the butt, but Bill had gotten used to him over the last four years. Was he with God now? Was he an angel? D-damn kid. He didn't like him that much anyway.

Then he heard his mother's cries and he thought his heart would break. He didn't dare leave his hiding place and go to her. She wouldn't want him anyway. Would she know what he'd done? Would his dad? He shuddered. Would they come and take him away now? Would they put him in the electric chair?

The hubbub below him went on for a long time. His mother's wails over Little Mack, the argument between Grandpa Sam and some strange man that came down the hill with her over who would carry Little Mack out to the truck and to the doctor, Uncle Jimmy smashing the shotgun with a ball peen hammer. Bill didn't dare move even after everyone left and it was quiet inside the barn. His heart thudded in his ears. He'd been crying a long time. His nose was so stuffy that he could barely breathe and his eyes were swollen closed. He curled up on the hay, ugly images flitting through his mind. Time passed and it started getting dark. The cows in the pasture lowed softly. They wanted to come in for the night and get milked.

"Bill?"

Bill woke up. It was RL's voice. Bill curled into a tighter ball.

"Bill? Are you in here?"

Bill couldn't bring himself to answer. Of all the people in the world, he loved RL the most. What would RL think if he knew what Bill had done?

26

RL opened each of the stalls before starting up the ladder to the loft. The floor squeaked. "You can't hide forever, squirt."

Bill opened his eyes. "How d-did you find me?"

"I already looked everywhere else."

"G-go away."

RL set a small basket on the hay bale. "It's time to come out."

"Where's M-Mama?"

RL took a sandwich wrapped in wax paper out of the basket. Bill's empty stomach growled when he saw it. "She's back home. Grandpa Sam chased off her friend and she's in bed now. They called Dad up in Michigan and he's on his way."

"Where's little M-Mack?"

"At the funeral parlor. Aunt Sara and Uncle Jim are there now too."

Bill sat up. "I d-don't want to go h-home."

"I told them Little Mack found that gun himself, Bill." RL handed him the sandwich. Cinnamon, sugar and butter.

"Why d-did you d-do that?"

"It was easier, but to be safe, let's tell them I found you in the tree house."

"Okay." Bill could count on RL. He took a bite of the sandwich and forced himself to swallow it.

"They are worried about you, Bill."

"I d-don't think so."

"I was worried about you."

The tears started again and he put the sandwich aside. "I d-

27

didn't mean to hurt Little Mack. I just w-wanted to p-play with the shotgun."

"I know, squirt. I was mad at first -- at you and Little Mack both." RL sat down beside Bill on the floor of the loft. "I guess kids are just naturally curious about things they aren't supposed to touch."

"D-don't hate me." Bill sobbed.

"I won't. I don't."

"I liked Little Mack. Really I did."

"I know. Little Mack was a great kid. Everyone loved him."

The three boys had shared a bed. Bill couldn't imagine waking up in the morning without Little Mack to kick off the covers and climb over him to go to the outhouse. "I w-wish it had b-been me -- then everyone wouldn't feel so b-bad."

"Ah, Billy boy. Don't talk like that. What would I do without my side-kick?"

It was nice of RL to say that but Bill knew better. "No one n-notices m-me unless I m-mess up. I'm n-not h-handsome and smart l-like you or c-cute and b-blond like little M-Mack."

RL's eyes brimmed with tears. "I couldn't afford to do without either one of you. What with Dad being gone and Mama being like she is, you guys are all I have."

RL was Bill's idol. He took care of everything. The world was upside down when RL was sad. "You are c-crying for Little Mack?"

RL put his arms around his little brother. "Yes, and for you and me. If I'd watched him better or if I'd come looking for you sooner, things would be different now. I'm so sorry, Bill. I let you down." RL hugged Bill and sobbed onto his shoulder.

Bill bit his bottom lip. It never occurred to him that RL

28

might think it was HIS fault. Tentatively, Bill patted RL on the back. "You d-didn't d-do anything wrong. I should have l-left Grandpa Sam's shotgun alone."

RL took a deep shuddering breath and stood up. "I need you right now." He held out his hand to help Bill up. "It's a mess up at the house. I can't handle Mama alone. Grandpa Sam and Uncle Jimmy and Aunt Sara are bad off too."

RL needed Bill? That couldn't be possible. He was a kid. He messed up all the time. He followed RL down the ladder.

"Poor Little Mack died because we let him down," RL said as they headed back up Bailey Hill. "You, me, Mama, Uncle Jimmy, Aunt Sara, Grandpa Sam -- even Dad up in Michigan."

Bill didn't know what to say. It was a scary thought. He relied on his family to take care of him.

Were they as helpless to stop bad things from happening as he was? The world seemed bigger and lonelier than ever before. Uglier too.

Colored Stones

Pittsburgh, Pennsylvania -- 1941

The young woman gripped her cardboard suitcase, searching faces in the crowd congregated inside Penn Station. Arty Lieberman almost didn't recognize her. She'd been round and bubbly and beautiful the last time he saw her in Mannheim. This girl was a hollow-eyed wraith.

"Gretchen!" His mother called.

"We're here. Over here." Arty waved his long arms.

Gretchen dropped her suitcase and embraced Ruth Lieberman. "Oh Ruth, I'm so glad to see you." She spoke in German, her Mannheimer accent quirky and comforting to Arty's ear. Then as if realizing that that part of her life was gone forever, she switched to English. "You look like great Aunt Margot and Grandmother."

Arty smiled to himself. He'd always felt a special bond with his German cousins. Their grandmothers were identical twins after all. "You look great," he lied because he didn't know what else to say. How do you tell a seventeen year old girl that she looked like a dried up leaf?

"I'm not ever letting you go." Ruth's hug went on for a long time. "Any word? Of Aunt Helga? Albert? Ilse? Anneliese? Hans?"

Gretchen's sobs exploded on Ruth's shoulder as though she'd held them back a long time. "Papa is dead. He shot himself rather than report for the deportation."

"NO!" Arty couldn't imagine the despair that would lead a strong man like Albert Weiss to choose death over life.

Ruth caught his eye over Gretchen's shoulder. She was shocked and horrified too but she kept her composure. "When did this happen?"

"Last year. October 20, 1940. Mama and I were packing when we heard the shot. The Nazis shipped us off to Gurs in Vichy France that same day. We don't even know what happened to his body."

In the chaos after deportation, did anyone say Kaddish for Albert, Arty wondered. To lie alone in some far off grave where none of your family could find you was too awful to contemplate. Arty knew exactly where he would rest when he died. His family had made arrangements with the synagogue years before. Even at fifteen, he found that comforting.

"Aunt Helga?" Ruth's voice trembled.

Arty knew that his mother was preparing herself for the worst. He held his breath, waiting for Gretchen's answer.

Gretchen pulled away from Ruth's tight grasp, her eyes glittering with tears. "The last time I saw her was at Gurs. She was sick. I didn't want to leave her, but she insisted. She said I had to go."

Arty blew air through his lips. His great Aunt Helga was still alive. He wouldn't have to tell his grandmother that her sister was dead. At least not today.

"Of course you had to go." Ruth took Gretchen's suitcase and handed it to Arty. "Think how worried your grandmother would be if you were still there."

Arty's relief melted into sadness. Since their last visit to Mannheim in 1935, the world had turned on their German relatives. First, the brown shirts kicked Gretchen, her sister

31

Anneliese, and several other Jewish children out of the Herwick swimming club. Although not hurt, they were humiliated and frightened. After that, Arty's father wouldn't let Arty and his sister Delores go back to Germany anymore. "It's too dangerous," he told Ruth. "Who looks at a passport in the middle of a pogrom?"

"A few kids at a swimming pool? It's nothing," Ruth had insisted. "Who said it's a pogrom?"

Arty figured his mother wasn't ready to accept what might happen in Germany. After all, her family had lived there for generations.

"And who takes a chance?"

Not Joe Lieberman, that's for sure. It was just as well. That was the year that the Nuremberg laws took effect changing Jewish life in Mannheim for the worse. Hans and Gretchen and Anneliese could no longer go to public schools or ride the streetcars or go to the theater. Mannheimers stopped doing business with Albert. Barred from the markets where she usually bought food, Ilse struggled to keep nourishing meals on the table. Great Aunt Helga withdrew and seldom left the house. Her letters to Arty's grandmother became more anxious.

To Arty, it was inconceivable that the Nazis would go after an old lady, but in the end, Great Aunt Helga disappeared along with all the other Mannheim Jews -- young or old. She'd been right to be afraid all along, Arty realized. "So you've been in that place all this time?"

"Mama and Aunt Helga and Annelise and I. Hans left for Poland shortly after *Kristallnacht*, you know -- after poppa came back from Dachau."

"It's lucky that we found you." Ruth patted Gretchen's hand. "When the Quaker lady called, I screamed to Joe and he thought I was crazy. Your great Aunt Margot was so excited she got on the phone with Delores right away to tell her the news."

"Thanks for taking me in, Ruth. I didn't think about where I would go. It was all about leaving at first."

"Shush. We are family. You belong with us."

"Yes." Gretchen sighed. "Family."

Arty swallowed. It was the first time he thought about how much that word meant to him. He had only been thirteen in 1938 when rioters raced through German cities attacking Jewish homes and businesses. It seemed too far away for Arty to take seriously until he heard that someone broke into Albert's store and the Weiss apartment upstairs, breaking or stealing everything in sight. Knowing that things he'd seen and touched had been destroyed, that people he knew and loved were victims made it hard for Arty to sleep. If he drifted off, he dreamed of Hans's glass chess pieces and Great Aunt Helga's collection of china spoons lying shattered in the street.

It was even worse when he realized that he knew some of the boys that beat Hans that night. One handsome young man had worked for Albert Weiss. Another named Eric was the son of the Weiss children's nanny. On his last visit to Mannheim, Arty and Hans played ball with Eric on the banks of the Neckar. It frightened Arty to think that old friends would turn on you that way. Every time he went into Pittsburgh he eyed passers-by wondering if they were enemies hiding behind friendly faces.

He shook off the ugly thoughts. Gretchen was safe and here with them at last. They should be happy if just for a little while. "Come on, you two," he said. "We're going to miss the bus back to Squirrel Hill."

"That's right." Ruth took Gretchen's arm. "We can catch up when we get home. I made a pound cake for you and there's

33

some hot tea with real sugar. We'll fatten you up in no time."

As they stepped out onto Grant Street, a gust of wind caught them. Gretchen's coat was too thin for Pittsburgh's cold December weather, Arty realized. Setting her suitcase on the sidewalk, he took off his jacket and wrapped it around her shoulders. "Don't want you to catch cold."

The jacket was huge on her. Shivering, she gripped the lapels with bony fingers. "You grew up, Arty."

He shrugged. "Happens to everyone eventually."

"The last time I saw you was when the Rhine froze over and we walked across it to Ludwigshafen. Do you remember?"

He remembered Mannheim vividly -- the *Wasserturm*, the odd horseshoe shape of the downtown area, the train station, the synagogue -- the unfriendly faces of a group of boys who chased him and Hans into Luisenpark. "I was nine years old and you were eleven. I pulled your braid and stuck out my tongue but you never told on me."

"Only because you and Delores were our guests. If you'd stayed another week, I'd have boxed your ears." She allowed her eyes to soften a little. "Where is Delores?"

Ruth sighed dramatically. "Off being a pilot. Can you imagine such a thing?"

Gretchen looked confused. "I can imagine many things."

The bus pulled up and they climbed aboard, glad to be out of the wind. "My Delores is such a wild, naughty child," Ruth said. "She's always getting into trouble even now. What kind of a woman prefers flying to getting married and having children?"

Arty smiled to himself. His mother and sister had fought over everything for years. Flying was only the most recent issue between them. How comforting the old family squabbles seemed in the face of the tragedy taking place in Europe.

"Maybe she could fly to France and rescue Mama and Anneliese and Grandmother."

Ruth's mouth dropped open. Arty smirked behind his fist wondering if Gretchen had always been so naive. "I'm sure she would if you asked her."

Ruth scowled at him. "They'd never let a young woman like Delores do that in times like these."

Arty wasn't sure who 'they' were, but perhaps his mother was right. As unlikely as it was that Delores could swoop down into a concentration camp and steal their relatives out from under the noses of the Nazis, the thought was comforting. He wished it was that simple.

Gretchen gazed out the bus window, tears trickling down her cheeks. "This is the first time I've been to America. We always wanted to come as a family, but the time was never right. I guess it never will be now."

"There's always hope until there is no hope." Ruth dug a handkerchief out of her purse and handed it to Gretchen.

Arty couldn't stand the lost and lonely look on Gretchen's face. It had been so long since he'd seen her. He'd forgotten about that little birthmark behind her ear. It made her seem familiar and vulnerable. He gritted his teeth, furious to think that anyone would be mean to her or hurt her in any way.

The bus left them off on the corner of Forbes and Murray Avenue. It was a short walk to the Liebermans's apartment. As they were climbing the front stoop, Arty's grandmother threw open the door. "Gretchen!"

"Aunt Margot." Gretchen ran up the steps and threw her arms around the frail white-haired lady.

"You're safe now, *liebchin*." Arty's grandmother stroked the girl's dark hair.

"Come on now, Mama. Let's get inside." Ruth herded them into the over-warm living room. "The poor girl needs food."

●●●●●

"I forgot what normal feels like." Gretchen ran her hand over a photo of Delores and Arty in Schenley Park. "To be in a real home surrounded by family. Aunt Margot, you look just like Grandmother Helga used to look before things fell apart." She pointed to another picture in the album, one of two tiny ladies squinting into the camera with their arms around each other.

"Helga's fine." Arty's grandmother squeezed Gretchen's hand. "I can feel it. Twins sense things about each other, you know."

"Your mother's fine too," Ruth called from the kitchen where she was making tea. "And Anneliese. We'll send money to bribe the guards. The Quakers will help us. You'll see. We'll get them out and bring them here."

Gretchen didn't look like she believed anything would ever be fine again. Arty wanted to reassure her, but he doubted if there was enough money in the world to get her family back again. He clenched his fist, choking back the passions that washed over him. "What happened to Hans?"

Even though it was warm in the little apartment, Gretchen hugged herself as though she were cold. "Hans is safe. He's in Japan."

"WHAT?" Grandmother Margot set up straighter.

Ruth stepped back into the living room from the kitchen. "He's where?"

"Kobe, Japan. In a Jewish community. He wrote to us."

36

They stared at Gretchen.

"What did he say, *liebchin?*" Grandmother Margot's hope soared. Arty could see it in her eyes. He prayed that she wouldn't be disappointed once again.

"He went to Lithuania when the German's invaded Poland. He wasn't the only one. There were thousands -- German and Polish and Lithuanian Jews trapped there with the Russians on one side and the Germans on the other."

"So how did he get out? A young man like that with no money?"

"He had Grandmother Helga's stones, the colored ones. Papa hid them in the heel of Anneliese's dancing slippers during *Kristallnacht.* We used the big sapphire to get him out of Dachau, but the rest Mama sewed into the hem of Hans's jacket so that he'd have money to travel and for food, so that he'd have a chance. Papa told Hans that one of us had to escape. Grandmother Helga was too sick to travel. Mama wouldn't leave her and I wouldn't leave Mama."

Arty glanced at his mother, leaning against the door jamb with a spatula in her hand. He imagined jackboots on the front stoop as the storm troopers came to take them away. He winced at the thought of them touching her, of her crying out in fear. NO! He'd never leave her alone to face the Nazis either. He shook off the image. "So how did Hans get out of Lithuania?"

"The Soviets let these people out through Russia if they could find someplace that would take them and someone that would give them transit papers." Gretchen accepted a cup of hot tea from Ruth and sipped it. "There were some Dutch Jews trapped in Lithuania along with the rest. The Dutch counsel agreed to give them papers for Curacao. Hans was lucky and got one too. Once they had a place to go, all they needed were the travel papers from the Japanese counsel in Kaunas."

"I didn't know the Japanese had anything to do with Lithuania." It was all too much for Arty. He'd never been very good in geography but it seemed to him that Tokyo was a long way from Kaunas.

"They were supposed to leave, but for some reason this man named Sugihara stayed for almost two weeks, handing out transit papers so that people could go to Moscow where they took the Trans Siberian Railway to Vladivostok and then a steamer across the Sea of Japan to Tsuruga. Hans said that he was one of the last to get out that way."

Ruth clasped her hands over her bosom. "There ARE good people in the world."

Arty imagined the Japanese to be tall and heroic. Clearly they were compassionate as well. Someday he'd meet that man Sugihara and shake his hand.

"We must write to Hans," Ruth declared. "It may take a while to get a visa given the circumstances but we can bring him here. He can work in the jewelry store with you and Arty."

There was hardly enough work for Arty in his father's store but they'd find a way to keep them all busy. Hans was older and had worked with his own father in Mannheim. He knew a lot more about jewelry than Arty did anyway.

"Oh Aunt Margot. Ruth. Do you think it's possible?" Gretchen's eyes flitted between the two women.

"Sure I do." Ruth smiled. "If the Japanese got him that far, I'm sure they'd help get him back with his family. Tomorrow is Monday and everything will be open. We'll start work on it tomorrow."

"*Danke, danke.*" Gretchen hugged Margot, stood up to wrap her arms around Ruth and then finally turned to Arty.

Arty stared at his mother over Gretchen's shoulder. So far, the only thing he'd done was share his coat and carry her suitcase. He was only a kid but surely there was something more he could do. Maybe he'd run away and fight with the British. Maybe he'd learn to fly like Delores. Maybe he'd become a guide rescuing people one at a time. Maybe, if his mother would let him.

"I have been much trouble to you. I know how expensive it will be to take care of me and find Hans." She turned her back to Arty and lifted the front of her skirt.

"We love you." Ruth wiped her eyes with the back of her hand. "You belong with us."

"Yes, but I can help at least." Gretchen's voice was muffled as she bent over, picking at the hem of her skirt.

Arty glanced at his grandmother who put a finger to her lips and shook her head.

Gretchen dropped her skirt and turned back to face them. "Maybe these will help." She held out her hand.

Margot struggled to her feet. Ruth leaned forward. Arty was tall enough to see the glitter in Gretchen's palm from where he stood.

"Hans has the colored stones. Anneliese has opals and gold. I have these. Grandmother Helga gave them to me for bread."

Ruth folded Gretchen's fingers back over the diamonds. "You should keep them."

"No. I was lucky. I only had to swallow them twice. I didn't have to use them at all. Things are bad at Gurs but I kept them safe. We will need them to get Mama and Anneliese and Grandmother out of there."

Margot held out her hand. "We'll do just that, *liebchin*."

Arty closed his eyes. It was the last of the Weiss family fortune. The damn Nazis had stripped them of everything -- their home, their dignity even their lives. He hated the bastards, HATED them. "Pop will get the best price." He couldn't think of anything more comforting to say.

Suddenly there was a commotion out in the street. Heavy footsteps thumped up the stairs. Gretchen hid behind Ruth, trembling. "LET ME IN! RUTH, LET ME IN!" Arty's father banged on the apartment door and they all jumped.

"My goodness, what's wrong?" Ruth opened the door.

"I forgot my damned key." Joe Lieberman was breathless. "Turn on the radio."

"Joe, we are spending time with Gretchen." Ruth gestured toward their frail guest. "Don't you remember she was to arrive today?"

"Welcome, Gretchen." Joe took her hand. "I don't mean to be rude, but something has happened. Arty, turn on KDKA."

Arty squatted in front of the radio and twisted a knob. After a few seconds, the tubes warmed up. At first there was static and then Arty adjusted the knob. " -- Harbor this morning." More static.

"What?" Ruth grabbed her husband's arm.

"The Japanese attacked Pearl Harbor."

"The Japanese?"

"Where is Pearl Harbor?" Arty twisted the knob again trying to tune into the excited voice talking about airplanes buzzing over the US fleet half a world away from Squirrel Hill.

"Shush." Joe Lieberman held up one finger. "Listen."

Arty's grandmother put her arm around Gretchen. "Why would the Japanese attack Hawaii?"

40

"NO! No more." Gretchen covered her face with both hands.

The news bulletin filled the apartment. Wide-eyed, they stood together around the wooden console, listening.

"Why are they doing this?" Arty's image of the noble Japanese who rescued Hans faded as he listened to tales of sinking ships and dying men.

"The world doesn't make sense, Arty. No use trying to make it so." Joe sank down on a foot stool as though someone had punched him in the stomach.

"What happens now?" Arty sat down beside his father thinking about Hans in Japan.

"War."

The Menagerie

Cleveland, Ohio –- 1942

Pam Kline squinted against the bright hot sun when she stepped outside the Terminal Tower. It was mid-morning on Public Square. Taxis, buses, trucks and cars filled the streets with blue fumes and beeping horns. She froze in the middle of the sidewalk, momentarily disoriented, as people swirled around her, many of them in uniform.

"Well, don't stand there, Goober. Let's go find us a circus." Danny gave her a little nudge. She scowled and pushed back. He might be all spiffied up and shiny in his sailor suit, but he was still her brother. The last time they came to see a ballgame, he was just a skinny kid in neatly pressed blue jeans and a baseball cap. That was only a few months ago. She'd never even heard of Pearl Harbor then.

They crossed the square and headed east on Superior. She struggled to keep up with him, a dog-eared copy of the *Ringling Brothers and Barnum & Bailey* magazine for 1942 under her arm. A painting of two elephants dancing was on the front cover. She wondered if one of them was Ringling Rosie. She'd never seen a real elephant, let alone an elephant ballet. She imagined them in their giant tutus twirling to the strains of a Stravinsky composition and giggled.

They turned left on East Ninth Street and headed towards the lake front, her excitement growing with every step. A breeze off of Lake Erie blew grit in their faces. They had money in their pockets. Since the war started, everyone had jobs again and their father's business was good. But they were planning on getting into the 'Greatest Show on Earth' for free -- Danny, because he was wearing his uniform, Pam because she would agree to crawl around under the bleachers collecting coke bottles dropped there by last night's audience.

The circus was set up on a lot not far from the municipal stadium, squeezed in between the bluffs below Cleveland and the railroad tracks. As elephants unloaded posts and canvas from the brightly painted train, large ships waited for wartime cargoes of steel in the glittering lake below them.

"Hurry up," Danny urged her as he extended his lead and disappeared over the crest of the hill.

"I AM hurrying." She ran to catch up, the calves of her legs aching. It wasn't fair. He always left her behind. He probably was meeting some of the guys down there or maybe a girl. He'd been sweet on Joanne Nelson for a long time but she never paid him any mind until he came back from basic training in his fancy white uniform.

As Pam fought to keep her balance on the gravely slope, she saw Danny leaning against a fence just outside the midway smoking a cigarette. A large poster behind him proclaimed, "One Hundred Clowns, One Thousand Animals." He waved and made faces. She stuck out her tongue and trotted up to the ticket booth.

"Ain't you a purty lil young'n?" An enormous woman in a flowered dress held a large roll of tickets. "Doors don't open til one o'clock unless you wanna collect up the empties. You payin or trollin' fer bottles?"

"Trollin'," Pam said and pocketed her pass. She glanced over her shoulder at Danny who'd been joined by another boy in a brand new uniform. Army, Pam guessed. The boys made whooping sounds whenever one of the circus women in their

43

tight fitting costumes wandered across the lot. She KNEW it. Danny had other plans. She kicked a piece of gravel and it went skittering across the road.

"Go on down to the big top, that red and white tent just beyond the Menagerie. You gather up the empties and put 'em in that striped box across the way there. Ya see it?" The ticket lady was nice enough, but Pam had never seen anyone quite so hairy before. One thick brow covered both eyes and she had dark hair on her cheeks and a thin mustache. There was even hair on the tops of her football-sized breasts where they bulged out of the neckline of her dress.

"Yes, ma'am. I see it."

"That sailor boy related to you?"

"Yes, ma'am. That's my brother, Danny. He's leaving for San Diego tomorrow."

"I ain't sposed to let you do this, but you tell him he and his friend can go on in with you if he wants. None of the sideshows will be open yet, but you can see the animals and talk with the circus folk after you are through with them bottles."

"Is Ringling Rosie here?"

"She's here alright." Several of the woman's hairy chins jiggled as she laughed. "Every body wants to see that sweet lil elephant. She's in the Menagerie right there waiting for her lunch."

Pam couldn't help but examine her own forearms for any telltale hair growth as she waved the two boys in. They crushed their cigarette butts beneath their boots and loped along beside her.

"Bennie Bermeister, I'd have never recognized you in that getup," Pam said to the tall, pimply-faced young man who

44

draped his arm around her shoulders. His breath smelled like sour chocolate and she wrinkled her nose. They were related in some distant way no one understood.

"How ya doing, half a chunk?" Bennie patted her head like she was a puppy.

She HATED when he did that. "Cut it out!" She pulled away and punched him in the side.

"You're growing up now, aren't you?" He pinched her cheek. "Don't you think you oughta trade in them overalls for a dress?"

She slapped at Bennie with both hands, dropping her magazine in the dust. "Take your hands off of me." He backed away as she advanced on him like a militant windmill.

"Aw, Pam, don't be such a stick in the mud," Danny grabbed her from behind, pinning her flailing arms to her sides and lifting her up off the ground. "Don't you know when you are being teased?"

"He ain't got no call doing me that way." She kicked and squirmed.

"No, he sure doesn't. But he's sorry and he's not going to do it again, ain't that right, Bennie?" Danny frowned at Bennie who flushed and nodded. "You gonna be good if I let go of you, Goober?"

"What's he doing here anyway?"

"I came to see the circus, same as you." Bennie tipped his cap over one eye and dusted off his hands like that uniform made him a big shot or something.

"Doesn't mean you have to follow us around." Pam had no use for Bennie. He had teased her since she was six years old -- taking balls away from her and holding them over her head, or kicking over her Tinker Toy creations.

"Pam, you behave yourself," Danny admonished her.

"I mean it, I don't want him around."

"Fine, I'll go look at Gargantua all by myself." Bennie turned on his heel and disappeared into the Menagerie Tent.

Danny let go of Pam and she turned on him. "I'm too old for you to keep holding me back that way, Danny Kline!"

"You're too old to act that way," he retorted. "I thought we were gonna have a good time and we ain't even in the door before you are picking a fight with Bennie."

"I thought you were taking ME to the circus." A tear rolled down her cheek. "You're going to war tomorrow and you wanna spend the day with HIM?"

Danny handed her his handkerchief. "I don't wanna spend the day with him, he just showed up."

She blew her nose. Her sock had slipped down inside her scuffed saddle shoe and she bent to straighten it. "Then let's just leave him here," she muttered. Danny always chose his friends over her. ALWAYS. She picked up the circus magazine, rolled it up and stuck it in her back pocket.

"All right. Let's go take care of those bottles before the sideshows open." He took her hand. She'd wanted to go see Ringling Rosie first, but she wanted to get away from Bennie Bermeister more.

A mild circus smell – fresh hay, even fresher manure, and overripe bananas -- drifted over them as they passed the Menagerie. A bald-headed midget handed them a flour sack as they went into the Big Top. Three other kids were clambering around under the bleachers to the left, so Pam and Danny started on the right. Cool air chilled their cheeks. It was air-conditioned. Pam held up her palms, turning slowly to feel the sweat drying on her forehead and under her chin. "I never been in an air-conditioned tent before," she said.

"There's lotsa places you never been." Danny held out the sack and she dropped the first bottle into it.

They worked for several minutes, filling the bag with clinking glass. She thought about Danny on a big ship halfway around the world. As usual, she was being left behind. What if he didn't come back? Maybe this was the last time they'd go to Cleveland together. Maybe this was the last day they'd spend together. Her nose burned and her eyes welled with tears. She didn't get it. Who WERE the Japs and why were they mad at them? And why did HER brother have to go fight them?

"Are you scared?" she asked as two men in glittery costumes shimmied up thick ropes to get to the trapeze overhead.

"Naw, not really." He swung the bag over one shoulder. "You set any bottles you find on the bleacher. I'll go empty this and come back."

"Why not?" She stuck her head out between two seats.

"I don't know." He shrugged. "Maybe cause it doesn't seem real yet."

"Yeah." That made sense to her. How can you be afraid of something so far away? She went back to work as he walked around the first ring to dump the bottles into the box across from the Big Top. A net swung under the trapeze where the flyers were practicing. That was good. It wasn't so scary with the net.

Suddenly there was a commotion outside the Big Top -- shouting, scuffling, and a shrill metallic screech. Danny was nowhere in sight. She got down on her stomach on the grass and slipped her head under the bottom of the tent. Someone's burning hot dogs, she thought. A canvas top shading

47

Gargantua and his mate connected the Big Top with the Menagerie. The gorillas bounced up and down in their cage and pounded their chests in alarm. Their handlers cut the lines with an ax and the canvas top dropped over their cage. Two other men threw water on them.

Odd bits of smoldering straw and blackened paper drifted down between the tents. Pam looked up. The roof of the Menagerie was on fire. A zebra galloped by. His mouth was open and she could see his quivering tongue. A burning square of canvas drifted down on his back and he bucked and kicked, braying like a donkey. The gorilla cage blocked him in so he spun in a tight circle and headed back in the direction he came.

Directly across from her, Bennie Bermeister crawled out from under the sidewall of the Menagerie. He looked left and right before standing up. She was right there in front of him but he didn't speak to her. He dusted the dirt off of the front of his uniform before strolling towards the lake whistling.

"You BASTARD!" She screamed after him. He glanced back at her and laughed, extending his middle finger, before squeezing past the gorillas and heading towards the railroad tracks.

She wiggled and pulled herself out from the tent as she'd seen Bennie do. The lake breeze blew her long hair into her eyes. Flames crackled in the tent across from her. Elephants trumpeted, lions roared. Someone hooked the gorilla cage to a tractor and pulled it to safety. Where was Danny? She ran around to the front of the Menagerie. Smoke curled around her as she crouched in the doorway –– stinging her eyes and covering her with a thick, waxy soot. Almost blind, she felt people run past her into the tent, others ran out with bawling, stamping animals on leashes. Heat seared her lungs.

An ostrich came at her, his feathers on fire. She ducked low and he bounded over her. Three men chased him down,

48

wrestling the big bird to the ground and beating out the flames with their hands. His beak opened and closed slowly. All along his back and up his neck, his feathers were gone and the flesh beneath was bloody red. Pam knew he would die.

A giraffe raced out of the tent, its bulk looming over her. Pam turned and ran towards the ticket booth -- the big animal close behind. Tripping, she fell hard, hitting her mouth on a small rock. She covered her head with her hands and the giraffe stepped over her body before wandering down toward the mess tent across the road.

She sat up and touched her mouth. A piece of her front tooth dropped into her palm. Her lip bled profusely. She touched it with her tongue. A giant came out of the smoky chaos and she rolled out of his path. He ran into the burning Menagerie bellowing orders. Pam covered her face with Danny's handkerchief. How could anyone run INTO that heat? A moment later, a line of elephants filed out, each one holding onto the tail of the one in front. Their ears were blackened and strips of flesh hung from their sides and backs. One elephant refused to leave. As the burning tent began collapsing around her, the tall man who was obviously the elephant trainer ran for his life, the side of his face covered with bright pink blisters. The last elephant swayed from side to side and wailed as the flames enveloped her. The camels all burned -- and the cats in their cages.

A shriek pierced Pam's ears. It went on and on. Animals and people ran around her as she sat in the dust and still the screaming continued. A white-faced angel dashed towards her. He floated through the clouds of smoke and grabbed her.

"Pammie, oh Pam." Danny picked her up like she was a baby. She wrapped her arms around his neck and her legs around his waist. It was then she realized the screams were her own.

The Menagerie was gone now, nothing left but the poles. Circus water trucks and Cleveland fire engines arrived and sprayed water on the burning elephant. The stench overwhelmed them, and Pam gagged.

"Oh God, that's Ringling Rosie," a fireman yelled as he directed a stream towards the injured beast who stood bleeding amidst the charred cages of dying animals.

"Ringling Rosie?" Pam lifted her head.

"Are you hurt?" Danny rubbed the grime from her face with his thumbs. She jerked her face away from him, trying to look over his shoulder into what used to be the Menagerie. "Stop it now, tell me. Are you hurt?"

"Ringling Rosie?" Across the midway, the suffering elephant caught her eye. Pam stretched out her left hand to the beast who lifted her scorched trunk and trumpeted.

Danny hugged Pam close to his body. "Let's get you out of here."

"NO! NOOOOOO!" She sobbed as he fought his way through the crowds of people congregating around the smoldering corpses. The big man was trying to chain Rosie so the veterinarian could treat her, but she swayed from side to side -- pulling away from him one moment, charging him the next.

"Do it, dammit. DO IT!" The giant cried and a shot rang out. Rosie fell, whimpering and squirming in the muddy ashes. Pam screamed without sound. After a moment, she closed her mouth and laid her head in the crook of Danny's neck.

"It's not enough," the veterinarian yelled. "Get someone down here with something bigger."

"I-I have a submachine gun in the car," a youthful policeman said, his Adam's apple bobbing.

50

"Get it, goddammit. Can't you see she's hurting?" The giant paced back and forth wringing his hands.

"I don't think I can do it."

The tall man grabbed the front of the policeman's shirt. "GET IT!" The young man ran back to where the police cars were parked.

"Can you walk?" Danny whispered into Pam's ear. She nodded and he sat her on her feet. "Hold my hand, Pammie. Let's just start walking towards East Ninth. If we can't get to the road, we'll climb up the embankment, okay?"

The young policeman hurried past them with a big gun in his hands. They passed the elephant conga line. The big animals were swinging their trunks and moaning while their handlers treated their grotesque burns. Pam stared in horror before looking away. They were several blocks from the Menagerie when they heard the submachine gun.

• • • • •

The train rocked as they made the first curve out of town. Danny put his arm around Pam. Her eyebrows and lashes were singed. Bits of scorched hair fell onto her lap. Soot and caked blood covered her face.

"I can't get that smell out of my nose. It makes me feel sick."

"I couldn't find you. What would I have told Pop if I'd lost you, if you'd been hurt or killed?" Danny rubbed at her face with the soiled handkerchief he'd given her hours earlier. "I don't think he could stand it, Pam. He's lost so much. I don't think he could stand losing you."

"I'm not lost." She looked up at him. His eyes were red and his blonde hair was almost black from the smoky grit and ashes. "I'm fine. I'm not even burnt."

"What were you trying to do? Save the damned animals?"

51

"You weren't around. I got scared and peeked under the wall of the Big Top when I heard the commotion. When I saw the Menagerie on fire, I thought I better get out of there." She remembered the whooshing roar of the flames and her sudden terror. "And then things just happened around me."

"You could have been trampled or run over." Danny blew air through his lips. "I've got to leave tomorrow. I've got to take you home and tell Pop what happened and then leave."

"Danny, I think Bennie started the fire." Pam wiped her nose on her sleeve. "He was in the Menagerie when it started."

"Bennie's a pain but he wouldn't do something like that." Danny was too good. He couldn't imagine someone he knew would do something bad. Pam admired him. She wasn't like that, but she admired him.

"I screamed at him and he grinned like he knew something no one else did. He didn't even try to help me out from under the tent. He just ran off. The BASTARD!" Pam had known tragedy before, but never evil of this magnitude.

"Why would he do such a thing?" Danny shook his head.

"Because he's mean. He's always been mean."

"He's only seventeen years old. He's a kid just like us."

"He's never been like us. He used to pull Taminee's tail. That's why she ran off whenever he came over. And I saw him kick the black rooster that time it turned up with a broken leg. For no reason. And he was always punching me when you weren't looking."

"That cat ran away whenever any of the guys came over, Pam. She didn't like the noise."

Pam folded her arms over her chest and stuck out her lower lip. "I saw him, Danny -- and I think we ought to tell someone. Call the Cleveland police when we get home, maybe."

"Did you see him light the fire?"

That brought her up short. "No, but I KNOW he did it."

"You don't know anything. You saw him leaving the tent. Everyone runs from fire, Goober. Everyone."

"I didn't."

"You should have."

"What about all those animals? The lions? That big bird? What about Ringling Rosie?" She thought of the flames reflected in the little elephant's eyes.

"Just because it was awful doesn't mean it's anyone's fault."

"SOMEONE did it."

"It could have been an accident. Maybe it was an electrical spark or maybe a lantern exploded or maybe it just got too hot in there and something ignited. Bad stuff happens all the time without it being anyone's fault."

That idea scared her. If it was someone's fault, they could tell on them and the police would come and put them in jail and then everything would be safe and normal. The idea that catastrophe could be a bolt out of the blue – as uncontrollable as a sneeze, that was just too much to accept. "It's not FAIR!" She wailed. Ringling Rosie had reached out to her in her final agony, reached out to her to square things. "There has to be something we can do."

"What? Accuse Bennie? You can't prove it. What if you tell everyone and the police arrest him and he's punished? What if they put him in jail for a long time? And then you find out you were wrong? Think about his mama and daddy. Think about his little brother."

She scowled at him. "But someone has to pay for this. What if it IS Bennie and no one tells on him? What if he does it again? What if he burns someone's barn? Or someone's house?"

"That's a chance we have to take, isn't it?"

"It's not fair."

"Whoever said life was fair?" The corners of his mouth turned downwards.

"It's supposed to be." She sniffed.

Sweet Tooth Tommy

Austin, Texas -- 1943

Tommy didn't dare look back. Looney Loomis wasn't ten feet behind them and boiling mad.

"I'm gonna beat the shit out of you, you thieving bastards," Loomis roared.

He was fifty pounds heavier and thirty years older than either Cliff or Tommy. All they had to do was keep going until the stupid son of a bitch keeled over and they'd be home free.

Cliff was several steps ahead of Tommy but already slowing. What an asshole, Tommy thought. What's the world coming to when a kid like Cliff Barton couldn't outrun Looney Loomis?

"Get your ass in gear, Barton." Tommy smacked Cliff on the shoulder.

The stolen tire slung over Cliff's shoulder slapped against the side of his body and impeded his normal stride. "We were free and clear, you idiot -- but you had to go for that candy," Cliff puffed. His round cheeks were bright red with what Tommy hoped was frustration. If it was exhaustion they were both screwed.

"I'm going to rip off your heads and stuff them up your asses." Loomis wheezed a few yards behind them.

"He's running out of steam. Keep going." Tommy's mouth was full of fudge. He had stuffed his pants pockets with the gooey concoction too. "At the corner, you go straight and I'll cut through that back yard. He can't follow us both."

"No way. He'll follow me because it's easier than climbing that fence." The boy was too much of a sissy for this line of work. Tommy was going to have to get rid of Cliff sooner or later.

"Fine. YOU climb the fence and I'll lead him down to the lake." Tommy swallowed and accelerated down the street, pumping his arms and lifting his knees high as he ran.

As he reached the end of the next block, he heard Cliff screaming as Looney Loomis caught him trying to climb over the fence. "What a dope." Tommy slowed to a saunter and fished another piece of fudge out of his pocket. Enjoying the exquisite pleasure of sugar and chocolate, he turned onto East Third just as a police car zoomed past on Congress Avenue.

Poor Cliff, Tommy chuckled to himself. Caught with the evidence looped over his shoulder, the big dummy was facing some heavy-duty charges -- stealing tires and selling them on the black market was no joke these days. He'd be in jail for a while.

Tommy headed over to Guadalupe Street where they'd left the car. He wanted to get the hell out of town before Cliff realized what kind of fix he was in and started blabbing about what the two of them had been up to the last several months. He got into the old Ford coupe and drove out of town keeping his eyes on the rear view mirror in case there was trouble.

He was halfway to San Antonio by dawn. Parking along side of the road, he got out of the car and walked a few feet into the grass to take a leak. He'd finished his business and was zipping up his pants when he heard another car pull in behind the coupe. He whirled around.

An old man stood beside the coupe with his head stuck in the passenger side window.

"What the hell are you doing with my car?" Tommy was outraged. How dare this old fool mess with Tommy's stuff?

A young girl sat in a rusty pickup truck parked behind the Ford. "Look out, Abner," she called. "There's someone here after all."

Abner turned toward Tommy and held up his hand as though to ward off a blow. "Stand back, asshole," he warned.

"Get away from my car!" No way was Tommy going to let some ratty old bum with the seat torn out of his coveralls swipe that coupe after what he went through to get it in the first place. The real owner had chased him across a field of vegetables with a pitchfork when he stole a cherry pie out of the kitchen window. To get even with the stingy bastard, Tommy had circled back to the barn and made off with the Ford.

"Well now, sonny. We're out in the middle of nowhere here and I don't see anyone coming to help you."

Tommy spit into his palms and clenched his fists. "You think I can't put down a scarecrow like you?"

Abner grinned. Most of his front teeth were missing. Most likely it'd been years since he'd mixed it up. Tommy figured he'd put the old fart down with a jab to the stomach followed by a quick uppercut to the chin. Easy cheesy. He was still figuring it when Abner grabbed him by the collar and slammed his head into the side of the coupe.

● ● ● ● ●

The sweet smell of onions filled Tommy's nose. He woke up in the back of the pickup truck with an ugly black dog nosing around his crotch. He groaned and pushed it away.

"That old hound dog just loves chocolate." The girl set a box of canned meats in the back of the truck. "He'll worry you to death until you give him a chunk of what you have in your pockets."

"Where the hell am I?" Tommy rubbed the bump on the crown of his head.

"Hell and gone again from the highway where we found you so don't think you are gonna take off running and get anywhere soon. Besides, Abner can take the eye out of a squirrel at fifty yards with that old rifle of his. I wouldn't piss with him if I were you."

Tommy sat up and looked around. His vision was blurred and he couldn't quite tell if the girl was ugly or merely plain. "Where's Abner now?"

"Cleaning all that crap out of the coupe. You ain't much for keeping things neat and clean, are you?"

"Hasn't been a priority." Tommy rubbed his eyes. The dog lunged at him again, getting a tooth caught in his trouser pocket and ripping it loose.

"You might as well give him that fudge."

"No way." Tommy slapped the dog away. "Let him steal his own candy."

She set a third box of food in the truck. "That's what he's trying to do, mister."

"So which one are you?" Abner came around the side of the cab with an envelope full of papers in his hand. "Barton or Hanes?"

"What are you doing with my stuff?" Tommy dove for the envelope but Abner lifted it over his head and stepped back. Tommy's hands closed on thin air. Nearly losing his balance, he grabbed the back of the cab but before he could steady himself, the dog jumped him again. "For God's sake, will you make this critter leave me alone?"

"Reckon you and that dog gotta work things out between yourselves." Abner chuckled and shook the envelope. "So which is it?"

"Hanes. Tommy Hanes." Tommy kicked at the hound dog. It avoided his foot. Yelping as though he was beating it with a stick, it took off running through the onion field.

"I got a draft notice here but no discharge papers."

Tommy shrugged and avoided Abner's eyes.

"AWOL, Private Hanes? Or dodging the draft?"

"I got flat feet."

"Sure ya do."

"It's the truth and besides, I gotta take care of my sick mother." The real truth was that Tommy hated marching, uniforms, guns and taking orders. It was too damn hot in the South Pacific and too cold in Europe. As he saw it, he wasn't really soldier material and war created opportunities for someone smart enough to stay out of the fighting.

"Well, now. That's a shame that she's sick. Where is she?"

"I'm not telling you where my mother is. What if you were to go rob her?" Actually, Tommy's mother had been dead since he was eight years old.

"You got a shit load of black market goods in the back of that Ford, son but I can't find one piece of paper in here that authorizes you to buy or sell any of it. No indication where you got it all either."

Abner had everything he needed to turn him into the authorities. Tommy narrowed his eyes trying to decide what to do. There was no gun in sight despite what the girl had said. Tommy lied often enough that he suspected everyone else of lying all the time too. Abner was a tough old bird, but like as not, he was too blind to shoot even if he DID have a gun. It was probably worth taking a chance.

"Times are tough. People sell stuff because they need money. I pick up things from time to time." Tommy tried to look around without turning his head, his eyes shifting from one side to the other. Acres of onions stretched off to the right. The fields were well tended. That meant there had to be a farmhouse somewhere. To the left he spied a rutted trail. That must have been the way they came in. If he took off in that direction, maybe he'd run into someone who could give him a ride or show him the way to the highway.

Abner may have gotten the drop on him earlier, but Tommy was young and strong. No way could the old man run him down if he got a head start. Abner's eyes gleamed with amused malice as though he knew what Tommy was thinking. It was almost a dare. The old bastard! Tommy jumped out of the truck and sprinted toward the overgrown trail. Ahead of him, the hound dog reappeared -- eyes glowing, tail stiff behind him. Tommy froze mid-stride, waving his arms to keep his balance. "Get away from me, you sack of shit."

"He ain't gonna hurt you. Just give him the damned candy." The girl grabbed the dog around the neck.

Panting, Tommy darted to a scrawny tree a few yards away and scrambled up the trunk.

Abner laid his hand on the girl's shoulder. "Let him go, Geneva."

The dog jerked out of Geneva's arms and took up its post under the sagging limb where Tommy sat.

Abner folded his arms over his chest. "Now there's a solution. From the frying pan into the fire?"

From his perch in the tree, Tommy saw that the old man had

stripped the Ford. It sat on its axles with the wheels lying in the weeds. Both doors were wide open and Tommy and Cliff's possessions lay on the ground around the car. "What the hell's going on?" Treed like a squirrel, Tommy felt bluster was his only recourse.

"Geneva and I are romantics, Mr. Hanes. We like to think we are the Texas versions of Robin and Maid Marian -- but with a twist. We rob from the rich and keep the proceeds for ourselves." Abner slapped his knee and cackled. Like he was the first to come up with that one!

Geneva sighed and went back to removing bags of sugar and boxes of nylons from the trunk of the Ford and loading them in the truck.

"I'm not rich. Why are you picking on me?" Tommy winced as Geneva found his last Hershey bar hidden under a blanket in the back of the coupe.

"Geneva and I were just gonna steal us a tire. The left rear there is going bald." Abner gestured with his head. "But we hit the goddamned mother lode when we pulled up behind you, boy. Enough stuff here to feed ourselves for three or four months and plenty of things good enough to sell for cash."

Tommy had intended on doing just that. "What's to keep me from hitching back to San Marcos and turning the two of you in? You must live around here. Everyone probably knows you and your granddaughter there."

Geneva unwrapped the Hershey bar. The dog whimpered -- torn between keeping an eye on Tommy and mooching candy off of his mistress. "Abner ain't my grandfather."

Unable to stand it any longer, the hound galloped toward Geneva, ears flopping, tail wagging.

Geneva broke the candy in half and stuffed it in her mouth. "He's my husband," she said with her mouth full.

The dog got down on its belly, squirming along -- begging. Tommy cringed at the idea of that damned thieving beast gulping down his precious candy. Geneva giggled and tossed the other piece to Abner. The dog's eyes followed the Hershey's arc. So did Tommy's.

"Geneva and I have been man and wife for about ten months now, haven't we, baby?" Abner caught the candy and held it over his head teasing the animal now writhing at his feet.

Dogs had no dignity. Tommy would have gone for the old bastard's throat -- or waited until he was asleep at night and peed in his boot.

Not as vindictive as Tommy, the hound watched with sad eyes as the candy disappeared down Abner's gullet before returning to sit at the foot of Tommy's tree. "That makes you all the more noticeable in these little towns. Lots of churchgoers don't take to old codgers stealing their kids." It was a weak threat and Tommy knew it. War made for strange bedfellows. All kinds of things that would have been unthinkable five years ago were acceptable these days.

"I haven't been a kid in a long time." Geneva took an armload of sheets and towels out of the trunk of the coupe. "I already lost a boyfriend to the Navy and a husband to a widow in San Antone. I finally found me a man who's not gonna run off and join the Army or bed down with the first lonely woman who bats her eyelashes at him."

Abner leaned against the truck and sorted through the sheaf of papers in his hand. "Where's this Cliff Barton? Or is there any such person?"

"Got nailed by an off-duty cop back in Austin."

"Right."

How dare this dirty rotten thief question Tommy's credibility? These two were lower than the low -- stealing a man's hard earned belongings just because they could. Eating his candy? What WAS this world coming to? "Believe what you want."

"Isn't the first time a fellow's been hit on the head for his papers. Especially since it looks like you've about run out of luck. You better hope that the next time the cops pick you up they put you in the work farm for a good long time. The Army's shooting deserters now."

They were not. Were they? Tommy remembered a Laurel and Hardy movie where the fellows ended up in front of a firing squad. The idea of staring down the barrels of four or five rifles made him shiver. "They got nothing on me."

"I hope old Cliff is alive and kicking." Abner stuffed the papers back into the envelope and tossed them into the front seat of the truck. "If he's dead, it might be pretty incriminating for a fellow to have his damned birth certificate. They still hang people for murder hereabouts."

"I ain't no murderer."

"They hung that Camp Swift fellow not too far from here last month for killing a little girl."

"I AIN'T KILLED NO ONE." All this talk about killing was beginning to get on Tommy's nerves.

Abner put his hands on his hips and stared at Tommy as though he were sizing him up. "Where were you headed?"

"Home," Tommy lied. "My mother will be calling the cops if I don't show up soon. It's my birthday tomorrow."

"I thought your birthday was in January."

63

"HER birthday. Clean out your ears, asshole."

Geneva dropped an armful of women's clothes on the ground beneath the tree. "You are one lousy liar, mister." She sat down cross-legged to sort through the tangle of brassieres and slips.

"Don't mess with that stuff. It's for my mother. For her birthday." Tommy shook his finger at Geneva. The tree limb creaked and sagged lower. The dog whimpered and stood up, eager to get at Tommy's fudge-filled pockets.

"You got one great big old mama if she's wearing THESE clothes." Geneva held up a brassiere with cantaloupe-sized cups.

"My mother's a beautiful woman." Tommy barely remembered his mother but he was incensed by Geneva's implied criticism.

"You're quite the mama's boy then?" Abner knew how to twist the knife in Tommy's gut.

"Yes." Tommy lifted his chin.

"Right." Abner chuckled again.

Tommy dug the last of the soft fudge out of his pocket. The dog whined as Tommy stuffed it into his mouth and licked his fingers. It made him feel good to disappoint the irritating animal even though it was Abner and Geneva he wanted to goad.

"Find yourself something in that mess?" Abner glanced at Geneva.

"These are fat lady clothes." She made a face.

"Then stow it all. We'll see if we can sell it down in Mexico." Abner bent down to pick up a slip and turned his back on Tommy to toss it in the truck.

Not one to waste an opportunity, Tommy leapt onto Abner's back and held on tight.

"Why, you little sonuvabitch!" Abner staggered as Tommy's weight pulled him backwards.

"YEEEHAAAA!" Tommy wrapped his legs around the old man's waist.

"Leave my husband alone." Geneva jumped up and beat on Tommy's back with her fists. The dog barked and snapped at Tommy's legs as Abner swayed first one way and then another.

"He ain't hurting me," Abner gurgled, trying to peel Tommy's hands off his throat. "Get out of the way so I can sling him loose."

Geneva squealed and wrung her hands -- leaving room for the dog to nip at Tommy's buttocks.

"You people are lunatics." Tommy shrieked and loosened one arm to bat at the dog.

At just that moment, Abner spun around. Tommy lost his grip and went rolling across the grass. Suddenly, one hundred and fifty pounds lighter, Abner fell backwards and hit his head on the tree.

"ABNER!" Geneva put both hands to her face.

Abner slid to the ground holding his head, his feet straight out in front of him.

"MURDERER!" The girl flailed at Tommy trying to scratch his face.

He ducked and grabbed at her arms. "He's not dead. He's still making noises. Look at him. He's fine."

She continued swinging. "Stay away from me."

"You're hitting ME!" Tommy pushed her and ran around to the far side of the truck.

Geneva knelt beside her husband and put her hand behind his head.

"Hell of a headache." Abner sounded like he was inside a box.

"You're bleeding!" Geneva wailed.

For the first time, the dog seemed to lose interest in Tommy's pants and ran over to Abner, putting its paws on his chest and licking the old man's face.

"Think I'm gonna be sick." Abner's face was white.

Tommy crouched behind the truck and peered around the fender.

Geneva looked up at him, tears rolling down her cheeks. "You have to help him."

"What am I supposed to do?"

"I don't know, I don't know."

Tommy stood up. Was the old man really hurt all that bad? Abner's left leg twitched, spooking the dog. Geneva put her hands on the quivering limb, trying to hold it down. "Please, mister. You can't let him die."

Tommy scowled. Why should he have pity for them? They conked him on the head and drove him out into the middle of a damn onion field. They took all the stuff he and Cliff had gone to great pains to steal. They ate his last Hershey bar!

"OHHHH," Abner groaned.

Geneva put her arms around his neck, covering his face with kisses. "Don't die, baby. Don't die. I love you so much."

Tommy was shocked. Here was a young girl pledging her

heart to a wrinkled up cracker with no teeth. It didn't make sense. He was young and good-looking -- well healthy anyway. No woman -- young or old, pretty or plain -- ever said anything like that to him. Abner might be ugly as sin but he had a woman. At first that made Tommy feel terrible and alone. Then for some reason, it made him feel good. "Let's get him into the truck. There's got to be a hospital in San Marcos."

Geneva sat back on her heels. Abner's eyes rolled back in his head. "ABNER!" She snapped her fingers in front of his face. "Don't leave me. I can't stand it if you leave me."

"Here." Tommy squatted down beside the old man and slid his arm under his shoulders. "You get on the other side."

Together Geneva and Tommy got Abner's limp body into the cab of the truck. Geneva squeezed in beside him and put her arm around him. Tommy closed the door.

The dog jumped up into the bed of the truck which was stacked with Tommy's stolen goods. Tommy wondered if the beast sensed that something was wrong or if it simply knew there wasn't any more fudge.

Behind the wheel of the truck, Tommy saw what was left of the coupe. "Shit." It was the best car he ever stole and he was going to miss it. Putting the vehicle in gear, he bounced through the onion field and turned around.

"Believe that ax needs a good sharpening," Abner mumbled.

Tommy glanced at Geneva. Her eyes were huge and her nose was running. What the hell was he doing? He spun the wheel to avoid an armadillo scurrying across the trail. Warning bells went off in his head. Any good crook knows you don't go waltzing into a town with an injured man, a young girl and a truckload of contraband without getting folks curious. Nosy people could mean a heap of questions he didn't feel like answering.

"I ain't staying around."

"Just get us to the hospital, mister."

"Fine, cause I ain't staying around."

They bounced over a small ditch. Abner's head lolled about like a rag doll's. The dog in back whimpered. A hundred yards down the old rutted path was a farm road. Turns out, Abner hadn't taken him that far from the main highway after all. San Marcos was only a couple miles beyond that.

"I won't tell on you," Geneva said as they pulled up in front of the hospital.

"I don't give a shit what you do."

Tommy got out of the truck and ran into the hospital. A nurse stood at a desk a few feet inside. "I got a man fell out of a tree outside."

She yelled down the hall for help and followed him back to the truck. Geneva had already opened the door and climbed out. An orderly came out with a cart. Tommy and Geneva watched as they got Abner out of the truck and rushed him inside.

Just as the door closed behind them, Geneva turned to look at Tommy. He waved and she nodded.

Now that he didn't have to watch Geneva's grief play out in front of him, he didn't really care if Abner died. They couldn't pin it on him. It was none of his business. He took a deep breath and turned around.

The dog stood in the bed of the truck, wagging its tail like they were good buddies. "I hate your guts," he told it.

It gave him a big doggy grin, looking around for its owners -- then back at him.

"You can't go with me."

Seeming to agree with Tommy's logic, the hound jumped down and followed Geneva and Abner's scent to the hospital door. After circling a couple of times, it seemed to understand that they were inside so it curled up on the sidewalk and laid its nose on its paws.

Tommy shook his head. What a weird day it had been and it wasn't even lunchtime yet. First Looney Loomis chased them after he and Cliff broke into the fat cop's house to grab that plate of fudge. The idiot didn't even realize they'd stolen the tires off his car until they were half way down the block. Of course, Cliff Barton was no great loss. The kid was stupid and stupidity was a good way to get dead these days. Jail was a good place for him.

Then things got stranger after he ran into Abner and Geneva and the chocolate hound. He hoped the old guy wasn't hurt too bad, but after all he and the missus had been intent on stealing Tommy's stuff. They got what they deserved.

"Good riddance." He thumbed his nose at the red brick building. Then he climbed into their pickup filled with black market loot and drove away.

He almost made it through town when he saw a cop in the rear view mirror. "SHIT."

If he'd been in the coupe, he might have tried to outrun him -- but Abner's truck was old and in bad shape. He glanced in the mirror again. The cop gestured for him to pull over. "SHIT."

Abner was right about a lot of things. The army had been looking for Tommy for two years. He'd punched a smart-ass sergeant and took off right after basic training. Now here he was sitting in a truck full of stolen food, clothing and tires. He sighed and pulled over. He'd had a good run. Nothing lasts forever.

The cop pulled in behind him and got out of the squad car. Tommy leaned over to pick up a large pair of women's panties off the floorboards of the truck. It wasn't something he wanted to explain. Something caught his eye as he sat back up, stuffing the voluminous cotton briefs into his chocolate-coated pocket. A flash of white on the seat beside him caught his eyes -- the envelope with Tommy and Cliff's personal papers. He glanced into the mirror. The cop was sorting through a box of Spam in the back of the truck.

Cliff was ten years younger than Tommy and not quite old enough for the draft yet. In fact, except for being in jail back in Austin, the boy's record was remarkably clean. Tommy thought about the firing squad. He didn't think they'd shoot him, but he couldn't take that chance. What if Abner died? The state of Texas didn't seem to understand Tommy anymore than the Army did.

The cop tapped the roof of the cab. "Name?"

Would it work? He was pretty sure that one town never talked to the other. Even if they did, HE had Cliff's birth certificate. He figured the chances were pretty good that they'd believe him over some country boy from Tennessee. After all, what was the worse that could happen to a guy with no record? Most likely they'd just hand him over to the military. Tommy snorted. He'd already conned the Army once.

"NAME?" The cop repeated.

"Barton. Cliff Barton."

"Get out of the truck, Mr. Barton."

"Got any candy, officer?"

Kendall's Dream Girl

Richmond, California -- 1944

Kendall Smith leaned against a tree at the edge of the yard, a cigarette dangling from the corner of his mouth. It was the second time he'd followed Faith Weddington home from the café. He first noticed her because she reminded him of the dewy-eyed brunette pictured in the June 1943 Vargas calendar he'd stolen from his uncle's garage. Wearing nothing but a grass skirt and golden flowers in her hair, the model looked like a sleek lioness eying her prey. None of the women in Richmond were quite so exotic or interesting, that is until he spotted Faith.

"You going to get yourself into a mess of trouble spying on people like that."

Kendall started and dropped his cigarette, covering his upper lip with his knuckle -- a habit he'd cultivated since childhood. "You scared the hell out of me."

A tall dark woman in coveralls stood in the road behind him, her kinky brown hair tied up in a bandanna. "I hope so. Now get your butt on out of here."

"Aw, Bitsy, I'm not hurting anyone." Kendall ground the cigarette beneath his heel.

"Someone'll be hurting YOU, young'n. Now get out of here before Bethena Striker sees you. She don't have a sense of humor when it comes to Faith."

"Why is that? It's not like they are related or anything."

Bitsy rolled her eyes. "Some folks is jes sensitive about other folks staring into their houses. Now you get on home. Don't you have homework to do?"

"It's Friday. No homework tonight."

"Then go home and eat your dinner. Play a few chords on the Steinway. People are going to start thinking you're a peeping tom if you keep on hanging around here."

Kendall shrugged and picked up his notebook. He took a step and looked back hoping that having had her say, she'd move on.

Bitsy raised her eyebrows. "Scoot."

"We're both headed the same way."

"You know better than that."

"It doesn't make any sense." Wasn't like he wanted to marry Bitsy or anything. What harm could come from walking down the street with a Negro? They had a lot in common -- one outcast taking pity on another.

"The rules are no different in California than back home in Mississippi." Bitsy waved her lunch box at him. "I don't want no trouble here. Them Rosies'll be heading on down to work in a minute. No sense in getting them revved up."

"All these stupid rules." Kendall kicked at a rock in front of him. "Can't do this, can't do that. Nobody ever says why."

"No they sure don't." Bitsy kept her distance from him as they headed toward the shipyards. "Onlies time the rules change is when folks need somethin. That's why all us girls is working. It won't last though. Once the war's over, they'll chase us back home."

"That makes sense at least. All the soldiers coming home will need jobs and we won't need more new ships then."

Kendall paused on the street corner waiting for Bitsy to pass so he could light another cigarette.

"That won't make it any easier for us girls who moved out here. What are we sposed to do when they fire us all?" Bitsy slowed as she approached the corner, looking around to see if anyone was watching.

"Get married."

"It's not for everyone. Take Bethena Striker, for example. That girl is gonna be single forever. She never gives anyone a chance."

Kendall made a face. "Who'd want to marry her anyway?"

"Take my advice and go on home. There ain't nothing for you at that boarding house."

"I'm in love, Bitsy."

"All seventeen year old boys are in love."

"No, she's special."

A woman came out of the house across the street and Bitsy accelerated her step. "Onlies thing that makes Faith Weddington special is that she's open to possibilities. She gives everyone a chance."

"Oh yeah," he chuckled. "I should be so lucky." He waited until Bitsy disappeared down the street before heading back up the hill to the boarding house where Faith lived. He wasn't sure what he would do once he got there. Other than the fact that he was a regular customer at the Café, Faith probably didn't have any idea who he was. That was one of the reasons he loved her. Even though their conversations were limited, she made him feel special. The way she looked into his eyes as she took his order, winked at him while refilling his water glass, smiled while making change -- made him think that perhaps she saw something besides an ugly kid with a harelip.

It was getting dark and the fog was rolling in from Potrero Point. The lights were on in the kitchen and he could see Faith making sandwiches for her roommates who worked the night shift down at Shipyard Number 3. Two girls came out of the house with their lunch boxes tucked under their arms. Kendall ducked behind a tree as they passed, chattering about a sailor. What was it with women that they liked men in uniforms? That was another thing that didn't make sense to Kendall. A guy could be the biggest nobody on earth, but the day he came home from basic training he was suddenly in hot demand by the local girls.

A tall woman with a long graying braid appeared in the kitchen beside Faith. They seemed to be having some kind of disagreement. He crept forward and crouched below the window. Their voices were muted behind the glass, but it was clear that Bethena Striker was angry. There was a crash. Kendall rose up to peer over the sill. The two women faced each other. A broken dish lay on the floor between them. Faith backed away, crying. Kendall clenched his fists. No way would he let anyone hurt his dream girl even if he had to wrestle a pissy old maid like Bethena Striker.

Bethena glared at Faith for a moment. Then her face softened and she was almost pretty. "I'm sorry." Kendall read her lips. "I'm sorry, Faith."

Faith remained silent while Bethena gathered up the shards of crockery on the floor. Bethena said something else. Faith shook her head and turned her back. Bethena sighed and tossed the bits of broken pottery into the sink. Picking up her lunch box, she stormed out the back door. "Fine. Be that way," she said over her shoulder.

Kendall stood up and watched Bethena disappear into the fog.

"What are you doing here?"

74

Panicked, he dropped his notebook and took off.

"Stop, Kendall," Faith said. "I know who you are."

That brought him up short. He covered his mouth and turned to face her. "How did you know my name?"

"I know your uncle. He comes into the café just about every day and he's always bragging about you. Says you are good enough to play for Glenn Miller or Tommy Dorsey." Faith stood on the back porch, hugging herself against the chilly evening air.

Kendall's stomach cramped at the thought of his uncle knowing he'd been peeking in this woman's window.

She sniffed, the tears drying on her cheeks. "Don't worry, I won't tell him.

Relieved, he blew air through his lips. "Why?"

"Wasn't like I was undressed or anything." Wiping her eyes with the back of her hand, Faith opened the screen door. "You must be cold. Come on inside. I have some coffee, believe it or not."

Kendall picked up his notebook and stepped into the warm kitchen. A half loaf of fresh baked bread sat on a cutting board on the counter.

Faith caught him eying it. "Would you like a cheese sandwich?"

He shook his head, but the smell was heavenly. "Do you have any jam?"

"How about orange marmalade? My granny makes it every year."

He nodded, thrilled to be in her house. Everything about her excited him -- the shape of her body, the color of her eyes, the texture of her skin. She was a goddess, the woman of his dreams, the only one in the whole world who looked and smelled and sounded this way. Wanting her to like him, he racked his brain trying to think of something interesting to say.

"Sit down." She gestured with her head as she filled the coffee pot with water.

Flustered, he obeyed.

"So why were you spying on me, Kendall? Checking to see if the rumors are true?"

"What rumors?"

The corners of her mouth twitched. "Don't give me that."

His mind raced. What could she be talking about?

She cocked her head and raised her eyebrows. "No? Well, maybe you haven't heard at that." She opened a canister and dipped coffee into the pot. "So why were you hiding in Bethena's victory garden?"

Should he tell her the truth? That he thought about her night and day? That he dreamed of pressing his mouth against her cherry red lips? That he wanted to touch her breasts? Would it embarrass her? Anger her? Beautiful women never gave the likes of Kendall Smith a chance. It was a fact of life that he'd accepted, but desperation made him brave. Closing his eyes, he took a breath and made a stab at explaining himself. "I-I wanted to see you."

"Selling something for school?"

He swallowed back his humiliation. "No."

"I see." She set the pot on the stove and turned to face him, a small smile flickering across her face. "So what did you want to say to me?"

Now that he was here, he realized how hopeless it was. "I don't know. I just wanted to come see you."

"Ah." She picked up the knife and cut a thick slice of bread. "You remind me of my first boyfriend."

Kendall perked up. "I do?"

"Lord, I loved that boy. Still do. He played piano too. He could make Stephen Foster sound romantic." She smeared marmalade on the bread. "Don't know where he is now. Left out of here in '23 right after we graduated from high school. Came back to visit from time to time -- until he didn't. Could be dead now for all I know. This war took plenty others."

Kendall accepted the bread and took a bite. "Is that why you didn't marry?" She'd been pining after a lost love all these years. That was sweet. He wanted to take her in his arms and console her.

"Oh, I got married."

His fantasy bubble popped.

"Twice."

He knew that a woman so much older than him wouldn't be a virgin, but he was unprepared for Faith to be that experienced, especially since he was so green. This was the closest he'd ever gotten to a full-grown unrelated female. Loretta Rae Lindsey had kissed him on the cheek when they were thirteen, but he didn't count that because she ran away before he could respond. It must have been traumatic though because it put Loretta Rae off kissing permanently and the word was that she was going into a convent after graduation.

Faith sat down across from him, her eyes exploring his face. Kendall flushed and covered his upper lip with his right knuckle. Her intensity embarrassed and thrilled him at the same time. Maybe he DID have a chance with her. The poor woman had lost two husbands. Maybe they died of horrible diseases. Maybe they were killed in the war. How tragic! Her suffering made him love her all the more. "What happened to them?"

"My first husband was my first cousin. Our fathers were brothers and they'd been estranged for years. We met and eloped during a family reunion that Granny arranged to get her sons back together. I was only eighteen at the time and pretty wild. He was ten years older and had traveled all over the world as a merchant marine. I never knew anyone quite like him. He could pick up marbles with his toes while doing drunken handstand push ups. Imagine. None of the young men around here knew how to have fun like that." She winked and Kendall realized that she was joking about being impressed with her cousin's antics. "At first, that put me off but he had a way with words. He could talk the pope into having a T-Bone on Good Friday. I'd only known him two days when he convinced me to give him a chance. We got as far as Phoenix before our Daddies caught up with us and had the marriage annulled. They are still fighting over it." She elbowed him and laughed.

Annulled wasn't so bad. Whatever the poor woman did with her first cousin didn't count. The church said so. Besides, they couldn't have had time to get too romantic while running away and all. "Where is he now?"

The coffee began boiling and Faith got up to lower the heat. "Last I heard he'd gone back to sea -- running goods across the Atlantic, dodging U-boats."

Kendall's hopes plunged again. How could he bat against a guy like that? The most daring thing he'd ever done was swing out over Miller's Pond on an old tire.

Faith took two mugs out of the cupboard. "I don't have any sugar but I have cream."

"That's fine." He hated coffee but he would have drunk motor oil if she served it to him.

"My second husband was in his eighties. He owned this house. He had a heart attack three days after we got married."

How could an old man satisfy a woman like Faith? He couldn't. No way. She must have been waiting for a strapping young fellow like Kendall all her life. Well, he was here for her. What he lacked in experience, he more than made up for in enthusiasm. "I'm so very sorry," he lied.

"Old Festus was the sweetest thing. I knew our relationship wouldn't last through the ages, but I'd hoped we would make a week."

Kendall imagined Faith dressed in black, dropping flowers into Festus's grave. How brave. How virtuous. How heartbreaking!

"Once he got over his heart attack, he divorced me and moved back to Missouri where his older sister could take care of him. The judge gave me this house and Festus sends me a check once a month, just like clockwork."

Kendall blinked. Faith was a divorcee? That would be a problem with his family. In his mother's world, there was something nefarious about women who couldn't hang onto their men. Apparently, their knowledge of intimate things compelled them to flirt with all the husbands in town thus aggravating all the wives.

It didn't matter -- not to Kendall. It was a silly rule anyway. What did it matter if Faith had been married before? It made her all the more intriguing. She knew things that Kendall could only imagine. "So why do you work at the café if this place is paid for?"

Faith sipped her coffee. "I'm saving up for my son to go to college. I fancy he wants to be a doctor."

Kendall knew that plump young girls often disappeared and came home a few months later willowy thin. Once in a while, grandmothers suddenly produced babies of their own even though no one ever knew they were pregnant. Then there were widows with children who never knew their fathers -- in fact, no one could ever remember meeting those fathers. The thing of it was -- no one ever TALKED about these things, at least not the people involved. Was this what Faith meant about rumors? Were people talking about an illegitimate baby?

"You look shocked." Her smile was tentative.

"I didn't know you had a child."

"The most precious thing in my life."

Kendall imagined a dark haired imp with Faith's almond shaped eyes. "How old is he?"

"Seventeen."

He choked on his coffee.

She leaned forward and peered into his eyes. "Ah, I wondered how you'd react to that."

"Why are you telling me this?"

"Because I'm looking for him."

His dreams cracked like a brittle mirror. "I'm not your son."

"No?" She reached across the table and touched his cheek. "Are you sure?"

"You know my uncle."

"But do you know your father? Do you look like him?"

He stiffened. "I look like both my parents."

She took his hand and examined his fingernails. "Maybe you do," she sighed.

He pulled away. "What happened to your boy?"

"I was going to stow him with Granny, but he had a harelip. I had no choice but to leave him at the hospital where I had him so he could get treatment." She ran her finger down the scar on his upper lip. "Before I could come back for him, he was adopted. I've been looking for him ever since."

"Lots of kids have harelips."

Her eyes traced his hairline, pausing at the unruly cowlick over his left eye. "Not as many as you'd think."

His mother was a round little woman who went to church twice a week and baked casseroles for the neighbors when someone died. She was neat and plain and perfect. His father worked two jobs and played cards with his uncle on Saturday nights. He looked just like them except they both had light eyes and -- no, he wasn't going to start questioning things. "I'm not your son."

"I see." Her fingers lingered on his face. "Bethena will be angry with me again. I have weaknesses that she can't abide. I look for him everywhere, you see -- and find him everywhere. She hates that. I told her about seeing you at the café tonight and we argued. She thinks I'm obsessed with a boy that I'll never find. Perhaps I am."

He avoided her eyes, hurt that the reason he interested her had nothing to do with his manliness and everything to do with his boyishness -- angered by Bethena Striker's intrusion into Faith's life. "Your son is none of her business."

Faith sighed. "It's hard to explain about Bethena."

Something in her voice moved him and -- just like that, in the blink of an eye, he knew why Faith had left her little son at

81

the orphanage -- why her elderly husband had divorced her -- why there were rumors about her. His cheeks flushed. "I didn't mean to pry." That was a lie too and he sensed that she knew it.

"It's not easy to be different, Kendall."

The rejection was complete. He was still curious about her life but something had changed. His hopes about being her lover were gone, of course. He'd clung to them for a long time but in a way, being without them allowed him to consider other options now. "I think I better go home. My mother will be wondering where I am."

"It was nice to sit and chat. All the girls work the night shift. I get lonely at night in this big house by myself. Perhaps you can come visit again?"

"I'm going into the Marines. I already decided to skip graduation so I'll be leaving soon." Actually, he wasn't even sure the Marines would take him. Up until now, all his thoughts had been on how to bed Faith Weddington.

She covered her face with her hands -- a soft hiccuping sob. "If only you were a lot younger or a lot older. Then I could be sure."

He pushed back his chair. "My family needs me."

She stood up and put her arms around his neck. His stomach hurt and he was afraid to breathe. She smelled so good, but he couldn't let himself respond. "It's possible, Kendall. You are the right age. You look so much like him. So much -- and then, there's your lip."

"No, I don't. I can't." He backed away from her embrace, covering his mouth with his hand.

"I asked your uncle if you were adopted the other day."

His heart thundered in his ears. "And he said?"

"He said it wasn't any of my business."

He sighed and picked up his notebook. "I saw Bitsy Shore tonight."

Faith's eyes were brimming. "I like Bitsy."

Kendall's real mother would have told him to stay away from Negro women working in the shipyards.

"She told me I should quit spying on you."

Faith sniffed. "What else did she say?"

"That you were open to all kinds of possibilities."

Faith ran her fingers around the edge of Kendall's ear. "That's not always a virtue."

Cordell's Luck

Camp Tarawa, Hawaii -- December, 1944

Lyndon Cordell was in a fine mood. He was a handsome man and he knew it. Slicking back his golden hair, he peered into a tiny mirror tied to a tent pole. "You and Smitty going into Hilo with me, Zim?" He rubbed at his shiny front incisors with his thumb.

Bill Zimmer lay on his cot with his hands under his head, staring at the roof of the tent. "Watching Ioké w-watch you is no fun for me."

Cordell tossed a rolled up pair of socks at Bill. They bounced off his forehead and fell on the floor. "I've told you a hundred times. I'm not interested in Ioké."

"That's not the p-point, is it?"

"I can't do anything about that." Cordell had been charming women since he was a toddler back in Indianapolis. It was as natural as breathing to him.

"Why w-would you want to?"

In fact, Cordell didn't want to. Things came easy for him -- so easy that he couldn't understand why they didn't for others. "So why don't you come to town and work on her?"

"It's h-hopeless. She's a head taller than me."

So what else was new? At five foot one, Bill was shorter than most women anyway. Being tall, Cordell couldn't imagine what that might be like but he knew there was more than one way to skin a cat. "You buy her a drink. Flash those pearly whites. Give her a little of that Zimmer charm. Bingo. You got yourself a sweet little Hawaiian girl." Cordell squared his shoulders and flexed a bicep. "Besides, she told Lieberman who told the Sarge who told me that she thinks you're cute."

Bill's face darkened even more. "C-Cute? Puppies are c-cute. I'm a M-Marine."

"Hey, pal. Cute's a code word for sexy in girl talk."

"Where do you get that?"

"My sister's girlfriends used to come over all the time when I was a kid. They'd hole up in her room and talk about boys. The ones they liked the most were always 'cute'."

Bill rolled over to face the tent wall. "It's not the same with Ioké."

Cordell put his hands on his hips wondering what to do. He'd never been jealous or lonely or depressed that he could remember and he didn't have a clue how to cheer up someone as sad as Bill Zimmer. Of course, Cordell never had anyone close to him die either. It had to be awful to lose your big brother like that, especially when you were thousands of miles from home. "Tell you what. We'll go to Hilo but stay away from Kamehameha Avenue. There are lots of other places. We'll get us a steak. Down a beer or two or three. We won't even look for girls."

"I'm n-not hungry."

"That's because all the mess sergeant serves is Spam, tomatoes and pineapple. Everyone's burnt out."

"I couldn't eat a b-bite."

Cordell was worried about Bill. The guy hadn't touched much of anything since they told him about RL. "Poor old Smitty hates pineapple." Cordell tried a different track. "He's

85

starving to death. Let's go feed him." Actually, Kendall Smith would eat road kill if you gave him plenty of ketchup and a beer to go with it.

"We'll steer c-clear of Jimmy's?"

"It's Christmas, Zim. There'll be some kind of doings at the USO. We'll go there."

Bill sat up on his cot and rubbed his temples. "I guess it wouldn't h-hurt to go for a ride and b-blow the stink off."

Everyone else had backed away from Bill's black mood, but something about the grieving young man made Cordell feel guilty. "Sure, pal. This might be the last liberty we get for a while. Better take advantage."

● ● ● ● ●

The truck was nearly full by the time Cordell coaxed Bill out of the tent and rounded up Smitty. They crawled into the back and settled in for the long ride down through the clouds to Hilo on the northeastern coast of the island.

It was a beautiful day. Set up on the old Parker Ranch on the slope of the Mauna Lea volcano, Camp Tarawa was the temporary home of the newly formed Fifth Marine Division. Training on the big island since late August, the boys had gotten comfortable with the area, spending money in the nearby town of Waimea or playing on Kawaihae Beach. Hilo was bigger and further away, perfect for a two-day liberty.

"Did either of you guys see who took that candy Aunt Gert sent me for Christmas?" Smitty asked once they were on the road. "I think that jerk in the next tent has been stealing my food."

"The skinny guy that just transferred in? Cliff Barton?" Cordell didn't like the guy either. He seemed older than everyone else and something wasn't right about him. Rumor had it that Barton had spent time in the brig but no one seemed to know why.

"It's not that I mind." Smitty shrugged. "I'll share anything I have with my friends. Of course, Aunt Gert never was much of a cook and taffy's not her strong suit. I just hate that he helped himself."

"Did you see him do it?" Cordell hated jumping to conclusions, but he was absolutely sure that Cliff Barton was the one raiding Smitty's duffel.

"Fred Hurley l-lost an engraved lighter last week and Doc Kline's been looking for some sulfa d-drugs that someone swiped out of his kit." Bill flipped a cigarette butt out the back of the truck. "M-makes no sense to me. We all pretty m-much got the same stuff. Why the hell steal something you already g-got?"

Cordell sighed. "It's a sickness with some folks. There was a rich old lady used to come into my dad's drug store and steal Kotex."

"That's disgusting." Smitty elbowed Bill and smirked.

Bill's smile was pained.

To cover the awkwardness, Cordell rushed ahead with his story. "My old man said that she probably hadn't needed them in years. Maybe she had a different use like polishing her silver or something. Even if she did need them, she could have afforded to buy the whole damn store, but every week or so, there she'd be pilfering the Kotex."

"You didn't stop her?"

"Naw, we let it ride."

"You l-let people get away with shit like that and they'll w-walk all over you." Bill was a scrapper, always fighting to keep things fair and equal.

Cordell didn't expect Bill to understand. Not really.

"We figured she bought far more than she ever stole. Didn't want to embarrass the old biddy. It was probably the only thrill she had left in her life."

The boys sat quietly as the truck bumped over the rutted road.

"That was real nice of you and your daddy," Smitty said after awhile.

"My dad's a generous old coot."

"Sounds like you love him a lot."

"Don't you love yours?"

The scar on Smitty's upper lip made his grin lopsided. "Hell, yeah. My old man's not ever going to get ahead but he's never behind either. Works his ass off taking care of me and my mom. I remember one time -- I was maybe six or seven -- I was getting into a lot of trouble at school. I guess I didn't want to sit still or something. Anyway, this skinny old maid school teacher told him that learning to play a musical instrument would settle me down. Teach me some discipline or some such shit."

Cordell chuckled, remembering when his dad bought him a microscope and they spent the summer looking at drops of pond water.

"Miss Grady," Smitty continued softly. "That was her name, Miss Grady. She wanted to teach me to read music on a beat-up old piano in the gym, but my dad wouldn't have it. He sold a piece of land to one of our neighbors. They'd been fighting over it for years. I know it like to have killed him, but he did it. For me. It was second hand but I learned to play on this beautiful piano in our own parlor. My mom said that she loved sitting at the kitchen table in the next room listening to me pick my way through Mozart and Beethoven -- but my dad never got to listen. Every night he was back out there working that second job."

"Parents are like that." Cordell leaned back against the side of the truck, lost in his own memories of family and home.

"Crazy old fart." Smitty snorted and shook his head.

Cordell elbowed Smitty who punched him back. A little embarrassed by his own emotions, Cordell lapsed into silence thinking about his own piano lessons. He'd tried it for his mother's sake, but after a couple of years everyone agreed that music wasn't in Lyndon Cordell's future. Despite his brawny good looks, neither was athletics. Fact was, Cordell loved mathematics and science and girls.

Smitty nudged Cordell with his toe and Cordell nodded without turning his head. They'd been so caught up in their stories that they didn't notice that Bill Zimmer had withdrawn from the conversation and was staring out the back of the truck. Cordell wanted to say something comforting but he didn't know how. Besides, it was a little late to notice the tears running down Bill's cheeks.

●●●●●

The bar wasn't much. It was away from the main part of town and it was unlikely they'd run into the lovely Ioké. Cordell and Smitty made themselves at home at a table near the window while Bill bellied up to a pinball machine in a dark corner. Cordell leaned back in his chair and thought about how much fun the guys were having down on Kamehameha. He liked Bill Zimmer but he wasn't much fun to be around right now.

"What'll ya have, Mac?" The bartender was a balding fat man with a towel over his shoulder.

89

"Beer." Cordell held up three fingers.

"You think he's okay?" Smitty nodded toward Bill who was pounding on the pinball machine.

"He just needs a break."

"Everyone needs a break -- except you."

Cordell flushed. "Cut it out."

"You got the magic, pal. When you walk into the room, heads turn. Most of us dream of what you got. That's why we traipse along behind you hoping some of it rubs off."

"Christ, Smitty." Cordell ran a finger under his collar. "Enough."

"Look at Zim. He thinks he has to keep up with you long legged bastards in order to prove he's a Marine. For every step you take, he takes three. I never saw anyone so determined yet he always comes in last and always will."

Cordell squirmed in his seat. Even though it embarrassed Cordell to admit it, Smitty was right. The cards were stacked against Bill Zimmer. Small, plain, uneducated -- it was a lot to overcome. In his place, Cordell doubted he'd have the grit Bill did. Troubled, he lit a cigarette and offered one to Smitty. "Life's a crap shoot," he said as he inhaled. "Who we get for parents, whether we are tall or short, smart or dull, healthy or sick -- is luck. My mother was walking down the street one day and a taxi splashed her stockings. So she went to a department store a couple blocks out of her way to get a new pair. Just so happens that my dad came out of the revolving doors just as she was about to go in and bumped into her. That's how they met -- an accident. If they'd never met, I wouldn't even exist. None of the things you say you admire about me have anything to do with anything I ever did. It just happened. I'm a lucky guy -- always have been."

The bartender brought over three bottles of beer on a tray. Smitty drank half of his in one gulp, wiping his mouth on his sleeve afterwards. "That's a depressing thought. If it's all a matter of luck, then why should any of us even try? We'll get what we get -- or we won't and we can't do a thing about it."

"There's no other explanation." Cordell blew smoke through his nostrils. "I get so many things I don't deserve. Zim deserves so much that he'll never get."

A young woman came into the bar. Looking around the room, her eyes rested on Cordell. The dimple in her cheek deepened. She smiled and wiggled her fingers. He touched his forehead in a jaunty two-fingered salute.

The bartender said something to her. She turned to order her drink. He nodded and said something else. She glanced over her shoulder at Cordell before crawling up on a tall stool and crossing her legs.

"Gorgeous." Smitty leaned his chair back on two legs and took another sip of beer. "And yours for the taking, pal."

The unmistakable feminine invitation was tempting. All Cordell needed to do was ask her to dance, flirt a little, ask the question. He'd done it a hundred times. He was a healthy young man. She was attractive. They were shipping out soon. It would be a long time before he got to spend time with a pretty girl -- especially one that could speak English. He started to get up.

The pinball machine went silent and the only sound in the bar was the hum of conversation. Bill Zimmer was almost invisible in the dark corner. His mouth was open, his eyes glued on the pretty young woman sipping her drink at the front of the room. He took a step forward.

"Uh oh, Zimmer's got it bad." Smitty elbowed Cordell. "Guess the lovely Ioké is history."

91

Cordell relaxed back down in his chair. It was a small gesture, but it made him feel good anyway.

Bill took another step. The girl leaned an elbow on the bar, turning to face him. He stopped.

"Come on, pal. Go for it," Cordell murmured.

The girl eyed Bill up and down. A heartbeat. When Bill didn't approach her, she shrugged and returned to her drink. Bill's shoulders slumped. He seemed unable to decide what to do next.

"Zim! We got your beer." Cordell held up the bottle.

Bill jerked as though someone had touched him.

"You're falling behind." Smitty's bottle was already empty.

"G-great. My throat's d-dry as sandpaper." Bill turned a chair around backwards and straddled the seat. Accepting the beer from Cordell, he took a deep drink. "D-damn, that tastes g-good."

"Nice looking girl over there, Zim. Why don't you ask her to dance?" Cordell gestured with his head.

"Naw, she's n-not my type."

"Oh?"

Bill sucked down half the bottle of beer. "She looks like my mother."

"Damn." Smitty let the front chair legs come down on the floor with a crash. "That's enough to scar a man for life."

"I didn't know your mother was a big blond, Zim." Bill had once shown Cordell a picture of a tiny dark haired woman. The girl at the bar didn't look anything like her.

"She isn't."

"Why does she remind you of her then?"

"She's good at showing a man the b-back of her head."

●●●●●

It was dark when the boys stumbled out of the bar and staggered down toward the beach. The waves glittered on the sand.

"I'm stuffed." Smitty patted his stomach and belched.

"N-no wonder. That steak was bigger than your d-damn head." Bill sat down on a big rock and took off his shoes. "I never saw anyone who could p-pack away food like you can -- n-not even RL."

"It's a talent." Smitty tottered toward the water.

"Oh God, it's so beautiful!" Cordell put his head back and both arms in the air enjoying the flickering stars above him. "Woooooeeeee!"

Smitty's knees buckled and he grabbed hold of Cordell's arm to steady himself. "I think I had too much to drink."

"No k-kidding." Bill stripped off his socks and rolled up his pants. Leaving his shoes on the rock, he stood up and made a face. "Jesus, it's cold." He cringed as a wave splashed over his bare toes.

"It's seventy-five degrees, you sissy." Cordell took off his shirt. "Think how cold it is back up on that volcano."

"I think I'll take a nap." Smitty toppled forward onto his face.

"How does that guy put away so much beer?" Cordell pulled his tee shirt over his head.

"It's too c-cold for swimming." Bill rolled Smitty over onto his back. "Besides I hate thinking about all those c-critters slithering past me in the water."

"You southern boys are so cold-blooded."

"All the m-more reason to stay out of the d-damn ocean."

Cordell slipped out of his pants. "Come on. I dare you."

"I c-can't leave Smitty. What if a w-wave came up here and d-drowned him?"

"Not many people drown on the beach, Zim."

"D-damned crabs will eat him alive." Bill nudged a tiny crustacean with his toe.

Cordell had had enough of Bill Zimmer. The guy was about as much fun as a splinter in the ass. Now that he'd had a few beers, it was harder for Cordell to feel sorry for anyone. After all, he'd spent the day trying to make things up to Bill but the little runt refused to cooperate. He'd been sympathetic about the dead brother. He'd put up with the whining over Ioké. They'd passed on Jimmy's to spend Christmas in a dive. He'd given up a shot at a beautiful woman only to have Bill turn up his nose at her. Now the guy was being a wimp about a little midnight swim. "Fine. It ought to be a lot of fun watching Smitty snore. I'm heading out for the middle of the bay."

Bill studied his toes.

Cordell wished he could take it back but the words hung there between them. "I'm sorry I snapped. I'm a little drunk and more than a little full myself."

Bill shrugged and sat down on the beach beside Smitty.

"SHIT!" Cordell turned on his heel and waded out into the water in his skivvies. "Here I am in paradise spending Christmas with a sad sack and an unconscious tape worm." As

94

soon as the water was deep enough, he struck out with a strong breaststroke. He tired about fifty yards from shore. Treading water, he squinted back toward the beach. He could barely make out Bill and Smitty in the darkness. He was sluggish -- weighed down by steak and beer and other people's problems. He rolled over on his back and floated.

The stars flickered overhead. It was the first time he'd been alone since he joined the damn Marines and he relished it. He thought about his mother and kid sister -- extraordinary beauties -- both of them. At this very moment, they were probably gathered around the Christmas tree drinking eggnog and eating canapés. When he got back to Indianapolis he was going to go to college. His old man would like that. They could change the name of the store to Cordell and Son. Or maybe Cordell and Cordell. Yeah, that was better -- Cordell and Cordell. He'd marry some cute little girl. Someone that would fit in with the life his parents had established. They'd have two children -- a boy and a -- the cramp hit suddenly. "ARGH!" He swallowed a mouthful of salt water as he doubled up grabbing his side.

Curled into a ball, he went under. Fighting the cramp, he stretched upwards and rose to the surface. "HELP!" He screamed. "HELP ME!"

The cramp hit him again and water closed over his head. His lungs were bursting but he couldn't get himself back to the surface. He tried to force his muscles to relax but even more of them tightened, increasing the pain. He sank lower. This is it, he thought. I'm going to die. The two idiots on the beach are asleep. No way could they hear him. As he spiraled down into the blackness, he thought of his father's face.

Something grabbed him by the seat of his skivvies. He was powerless to move. He merely floated in the salty darkness feeling himself being pulled butt-first to the surface. As his head emerged from the water, he opened his mouth wide and sucked in as much air as he could.

"Goddammit, Cordell. You scared the shit out of me."

It was Bill's voice but there wasn't a hint of a stutter.

"Where are you, Zim?"

"You stupid sonuvabitch." Bill was somewhere behind him.

"What's going on?" Cordell swallowed more water and choked.

"Shut your damn mouth." Bill kicked and Cordell felt himself being towed backwards toward shore.

"HERE! OVER HERE!" It was Smitty's voice.

Cordell felt sand under his feet and he struggled to stand up. "I'm okay," he wheezed. "Let go of me, Zim."

Bill let go of the back of Cordell's skivvies and stood up himself. "You crazy bastard." Bill was shivering.

"Here, pal." Smitty helped Cordell out of the water. "Are you okay?"

"I don't know." He clutched his lower abdomen coughing. "Just a snoot full of water and a cramp."

Bill staggered over to the rock where he'd left his shoes and sat down, covering his face with his hands. "You goddamned idiot nearly got me killed."

Smitty slapped Bill on the back. "Damn, Zim! You're a frigging hero."

Cordell puked seawater onto the sand.

Bill peered between his fingers.

"Is that sonuvabitch okay?"

"He's fine. His ass is hanging out. You about ripped his

underwear off him but he's alive and well."

Cordell moaned and flopped down on the beach.

Smitty folded his arms over his chest and chuckled. "Maybe not perfect yet but he's gonna be. I'm amazed that you heard him."

"I c-can't b-believe I did."

"The old Cordell luck held I guess."

"Come on, Smitty." Cordell rolled over on his back and groaned. "If my luck had held I wouldn't have gotten in trouble in the first place."

Smitty helped Cordell to his feet. "You could be dead now if it weren't for Zim."

Cordell knew that was true. He outweighed Bill by at least eighty pounds. Somehow tiny Bill Zimmer had pulled him out of a bad spot. What were the odds of that? He limped over to the rock where Bill sat panting and held out his hand. "You saved me, Zim."

Bill stared at Cordell's hand like it was a sharp-toothed eel about to bite him.

"You saved my life," Cordell repeated.

Bill shook his head. "I c-couldn't have."

Cordell picked up his shirt which was lying on the beach where he'd dropped it only a few minutes before. A little damp and a little sandy, it was still dryer than Bill's clothes. "I'm telling you, pal. I was a dead man. You swam out and rescued me." Cordell wrapped his shirt around Bill's chilled body.

"You d-don't understand."

"What don't I understand?" The reality of what happened was beginning to register. Bill Zimmer was only at

97

the beach because Cordell had insisted that he come to Hilo. He'd stopped drinking hours before -- switching to a coke with dinner. Still depressed, the little guy hadn't been in the mood to eat much either. All the tiles had fallen in place. God had protected Cordell once again -- putting the right man in the right place at the right time. A strong man -- a determined one -- one who never gave up regardless of the odds -- hallelujah. Who would have thought that man would be Bill Zimmer?

"You should be d-dead."

"I was lucky you didn't pass out with Smitty or I would be." Cordell didn't believe in coincidences. This was a sign that he was supposed to survive the war. He was supposed to go home and run Cordell and Cordell Drug Store. Maybe he'd be mayor of Indianapolis some day. Maybe he'd be President of the United States. Anything was possible for a lucky man.

"N-no, it's n-not that." Bill looked like he was going to cry again.

"What then?" Smitty folded his arms over his chest and raised one eyebrow.

"I c-can't swim."

Iwo Jima

Iwo Jima, The Pacific

February – March, 1945

Chapter 1 -- At Sea

Bill Zimmer stood on tiptoe and leaned over the railing to watch the pale waves thrown up by the bow. The armada surrounded them, hundreds of ship-shaped shadows in the gloom. Spooked by the glittering black sea, he shivered and turned up his collar. "H-how m-much longer?"

"We must be getting close -- maybe a day or two out. Then it's the big show." Arty Lieberman's cigarette glowed in the darkness. Bill felt comfortable around Arty, as if he'd known him all his life. Maybe it was because Arty reminded him of RL. Of course, everything reminded Bill of RL these days.

The ship bounced over the waves and Kendall Smith gagged. "War or no war -- I want off this damn ship."

Poor Smitty had been seasick all the way from Pearl -- when he wasn't puking, he was talking about puking. It drove everyone crazy, especially Bill who couldn't stand the sight of blood or vomit or excrement. "My b-birthday was last week," he said to change the subject.

"How old?" Arty said, taking a final puff from his cigarette.

"Eighteen."

"I'll be nineteen next month if I make it." Arty blew smoke through his nostrils and pitched the butt into the sea.

"You're too young to talk like that." Squatting on the deck beside them, Sergeant Emil Kroner rattled the dice in his fist and tossed it against the bulkhead. "YEAH!"

Cordell groaned as Kroner gathered up a small pile of greenbacks and stuffed them into his pants.

"You ready to go again?"

Cordell turned his pockets inside out. "I'm busted."

"Let this be a lesson to you then. Lay off the craps." Kroner stood up and dusted off the seat of his uniform. "You'll see. The lot of you will go home and get married after we settle this score with the Japs so don't fritter away your money gambling. You're going to need it to support your lady loves."

"My mother will be glad to hear that," Arty said. "She's got her heart set on being a grandmother."

"Mothers are like that." Kroner leaned against the rail next to Bill and Arty.

Bill forgot about what lay in front of them for a moment and thought about home and his own mother. "I got m-me some running around to do first."

"What kind of gal did you have in mind, Zim?" Kroner winked at Cordell.

"Someone proper and sweet. I don't w-want any of them WACS or those tramps that w-wear slacks and work in the factories."

"You got that right." Smitty stared at the choppy water and swallowed several times.

"You guys have a lot of expectations. No one's perfect." Cordell pocketed the dice. When he stood up, he towered over Bill. Broad shouldered and handsome, Cordell was taller than any of them except Arty. Guys like him could take their pick. It was hard for Bill not to feel jealous of that, still he couldn't' help but like Cordell. They all did.

"I just w-want one that will be all m-mine. I don't want to think anyone else g-got there first. Some guys don't m-mind a used car, but I like n-new ones."

"So what kind of a car do you drive now?" Kroner raised one bushy eyebrow.

Stung, Bill blushed. "A used 1937 Buick."

They all laughed, including Bill. The Sarge sure knew how to make a fellow feel better. Women and cars worked lots better than thinking about your mother at a time like this.

The horizon lit up and thunderous waves of sound buffeted the ship. Smitty staggered back from the railing, eyes wide. "What the hell is THAT?"

"The bombardment." Kroner put his hand on Kendall Smith's shoulder. "It's okay, Smitty. You're safe. Those guns are pointed towards the island. It's not a good day to be a Jap though."

"We m-must be close if we can see it." The reality of their mission began to dawn on Bill. The flashes grew bigger and the noise louder as new guns joined the fray. Filled with dread, he inched backwards wondering if there was some place on the ship where he could hide until the whole thing was over.

"Poor bastards. How could anyone survive that?" Arty looked around as if he suddenly realized Bill was gone.

Pressing against a stack of crates on the deck, Bill flinched with the next explosion. Arty smiled and waved him back as though losing your nerve was no big deal. Bill gritted his teeth and nodded. If Arty could handle it, he supposed he could.

"You better hope the Navy slams the hell out of 'em, Lieberman. If the big guns don't get them, we'll have to," Kroner said.

Hoping that no one but Arty had noticed his moment of anxiety, Bill rejoined the rest of his squad at the rail. "How long are they going to b-blast them?" He said to cover his embarrassment.

"From now till we land." Kroner made room for him. "Let's hope it does the job."

"What's the n-name of that godforsaken place?"

"Iwo Jima."

The young Marines eyed each other, digesting this news.

"I never heard of it." Cordell echoed Bill's thoughts.

"We need it if we are going to take the mainland of Japan. At least that's what they told me at the briefing." Kroner raised his voice so that everyone lined up at the railing could hear him. "We need a place for the fly boys to refuel. Iwo is the best place for that so they've sent us to get it for them."

They all nodded.

"I just hope I don't get m-my ass shot off on some little island I never heard of," Bill whispered to Arty.

"No one's gonna shoot your sorry ass, Zim. It's not big enough to make a decent target."

The ship shuddered and the boys struggled to keep their balance. Cordell ducked as though the shell was coming his way. "Damn, they musta hit something big with that one."

"Hope they blow the shit out of them." Kroner cleared his sinuses and spit into the ocean.

"You ever been in a battle before, Sarge?"

"A couple."

"What's it like?"

All four boys turned to look at Kroner.

"Hell." Kroner stared out to sea. "It's like hell."

Chapter 2 -- The Night Before

Bill sat cross-legged on the floor of the crowded sleeping quarters. "I don't know if I can sleep."

"Not many can rest the night before an invasion, son." Captain Reese's voice was low and mellow like he wasn't scared of anything. "Do the best you can. The chaplain is conducting a Sunday evening service up on deck in a half hour, if you want. If not, I suggest you finish writing your folks in the next hour or so, and then it'll be lights out."

Bill hoped the Captain didn't really mean that. He watched Reese make his way through groups of anxious young men -- pausing to chat here, shaking a hand there. It was too little too late. The man had never spoken to him before. It was nice of him to try, of course -- but it was hard for Bill to take much comfort from a stranger.

He sighed and focused on the notepaper in his lap. 'Dear Mom,' he'd written. Now what? He imagined her face. What would she want to hear? That he was scared? That he missed RL as much as she did? It had been so long since he'd seen her. He couldn't remember if that little mole next to her mouth was on the right or left side. His own mother and he couldn't remember something as simple as that. He did remember her cinnamon, sugar and butter sandwiches though -- and her perfume and her tiny high heeled shoes. He laid down his pen. "I don't know what to say."

"Tell her you are having a lovely time and you wish she was

here." Cordell shouted from his hammock across a small aisle in the middle of the room.

"Yeah, I'll tell her that." Bill laughed. Cordell was a character -- he'd give him that. "What are you telling your folks? Met Betty Grable in Hawaii, we are now on a nice cruise?"

"Me and Betty are close." Cordell held two fingers together to indicate the nature of his intimacy with the lovely actress. "Maybe I'll write HER a letter instead of my mom."

"I think you b-better write your mom. She'll open the envelope at least."

Kendall Smith staggered down the aisle, clutching his stomach.

"Damn, Smitty. You look like shit." Cordell tossed a rolled up pair of socks at him.

"Doc K-Kline couldn't help?" Bill felt bad for Smitty. The two of them got to be buddies at Pendleton. Maybe it was because they were younger and smaller than the other guys. Maybe because neither of them ever had much luck with women and ended up going back to the base together after a night of drinking.

"He said he knew what to do if I got my ass shot off or if I had a fever. They didn't teach him much about bad bellies." Smitty grabbed a pole to steady himself as the ship lurched.

"You n-never had a problem eating before." Back in Hilo, Bill once watched Smitty eat three steak dinners and down enough beer to make a whole squad sick.

"Maybe it's nerves?" Arty dangled his long legs over the edge of his hammock and rummaged through his knapsack. "Did anyone see a chain with a medal on it?"

"Of course, it's nerves. It's always nerves, but how the hell

105

do I get rid of them?" Smitty was pale as a ghost.

"I got something that might help." Cordell jumped down out of his bunk and rummaged through his duffle.

"Oh sure. If Doc Kline can't help, how can you?"

"My dad's a pharmacist back in Indianapolis." Cordell took out a small bottle. He laid a sheet of writing paper flat on his hammock and poured out a small mound of white powder. "Mix it with a little water and drink it down. It's just the thing to make you feel better."

Smitty stared at the paper in the palm of Cordell's hand. "How do you know about stomach medicine if Doc Kline doesn't?"

"I told you. My dad's a pharmacist."

"That doesn't mean YOU are." Smitty poked at the mound of powder with his forefinger.

Cordell shrugged. "I've used this stuff for years."

"You aren't going to poison me?"

"Do I look poisoned?" Cordell squared his shoulders. He was rosy cheeked and blooming with health.

"You don't ever see Cordell puking his guts out." Arty had his arm in his duffle pulling out rolled up clothes, shoes and books.

"It c-can't hurt." Smitty's belches and farts entertained them during the day and tainted their air at night. Everyone wanted the poor guy's stomach to settle down, especially Bill who had a hard time dealing with sick people.

"Take it, Smitty." Cordell folded the paper into a small envelope and slipped it into Smitty's shirt pocket. "If you don't want to take it now, keep it with you for future belly aches."

"Thanks." Bill thought Smitty seemed embarrassed.

• • • • •

"I still have to write this letter." Bill tapped his pencil against the blank sheet of paper.

"I'm having a hard time too, Zim." Arty lay on his stomach, his head over the edge of his hammock looking down at Bill on the floor below. He'd given up trying to find his medal. It was too bad. Bill knew it meant a lot to Arty.

"Are you s-scared?" Bill lowered his voice to a whisper.

"Damned right I'm scared -- aren't you?"

Bill ducked his head.

"Don't worry, buddy. Everyone with a lick of sense is scared, even old Cordell over there. He just does a better job of hiding it than the rest of us."

"I k-keep thinking about my b-brother. Didn't nothing scare him."

"You and RL were pretty tight, weren't you?"

Bill kept his eyes on the letter in his lap. "Everybody loved RL."

"What did RL stand for?"

"Robert Lee. Like that Civil War General. Every other kid in the south is n-named after him. My m-mom -- she's n-nuts. She thinks that the Confederates really w-won that war."

Arty laughed. "So how does she figure that you are fighting for the United States now?"

Bill shrugged. "I t-told you. She's crazy."

"Lots of that around. My grandmother spits between her fingers to keep evil spirits away."

"Does it w-work?"

"Well, considering what Hitler is doing to the world, I'd guess it's not too effective."

"I don't know m-much about that. Didn't get p-past the eighth grade. I joined up b-because they were going to d-draft m-me if I didn't."

"I think we are doing something important here. The Nazis got some of my relatives in Europe so I wish I was over there, of course."

"So why the hell did you become a M-Marine? That's an army show over there."

"Hell, I was only seventeen when I signed up. I didn't know what I was doing." Arty rolled onto his back and dangled his long legs over either side of his bed. "Damn, I was stupid."

Bill didn't think Arty was stupid at all. There was more to that story but Bill was willing to accept Arty's version of things. It was the least a guy could do for a buddy. "I did it on a d-dare. I wanted to show them a little bitty guy like me can be as good a M-Marine as any of them."

"Who were you gonna show, Zim?"

"Some big six foot b-bastard standing in line with me."

"What happened to him? Did you show him?"

"He didn't p-pass the physical. He's probably b-back home working in a factory somewhere, getting laid twice a week."

"Ain't we a pair? We're gonna get our asses shot off tomorrow because of stupidity and pride."

"I want to g-get it over with. I'm tired of this rickety old ship. I thought it was bad c-coming out from Pendleton, but this last ride's b-been worse. I hate being c-cooped up. I hate that every time I turn around something else is missing out of my stuff. I hate smelling Smitty's d-dirty socks. I hate the ocean, especially at night. It's dark and c-cold and there are all k-kinds of things in it." He shuddered. "It's m-moving all the time too. I never know what to expect. I'm from Arkansas. The ground doesn't m-move. It's solid -- it doesn't tip our h-house on its side or threaten to swallow it up."

"Don't be so eager, Zim. Up to now, it's been like a rough version of boy scouts, hanging out with the guys, camping, playing war games. Tomorrow will be different."

It scared Bill to hear Arty talk that way. "How ya m-mean?"

"You religious, Zim?"

"I don't know. I g-go to church sometimes. Baptist."

"Well, when you are Jewish, you have a bar mitzvahs. That's a ceremony when you are thirteen. After your bar mitzvahs, you are considered a man."

"One day you are a k-kid, the next a man?" Arty was the first Jew Bill had ever met.

"After tomorrow, I think we'll be different -- just like that."

"B-Because we will have k-killed us some Japs? They are the enemy, Arty. They ain't hardly human. They don't think like us. Everyone says so. Besides, they are going to be trying to k-kill us. It's them or us." Bill planned on doing everything he could to stay alive. He'd promised his mother he would.

"There are some things I'm scared of knowing, Zim."

Sometimes Arty thought too much. "Think about b-being a hero," Bill said. "We'll get us some m-medals. When we go home, we'll have to b-beat women off with a stick."

"A hero? Hmm."

"I think this is my chance, m-maybe the only one I'm ever gonna get. RL took care of things. Now that he's dead, I gotta d-do it myself." Bill sniffed -- rubbed his nose -- sniffed again. "My m-mom's probably all t-tore up. He was her favorite, you know. I w-wanna do something to make her proud, maybe m-make up for RL being dead and all."

"She's already proud of you, Zim." Arty put his arms behind his head and stared at the hammock above him.

Bill doubted that was true but it was nice of Arty to say it. "I still don't know w-what to write."

"How about this. Dear Mom, I'm doing fine. Tomorrow is a big day. I love you. Bill."

"That sounds about right." Bill wrote the words in an awkward, childish scrawl. He folded the letter into an envelope and sealed it.

A broad shouldered boy tapped Arty on the shoulder. "Going up to the service, Lieberman?"

Bill didn't know Kirby very well. He wasn't part of Kroner's unit in the beginning. He and his buddies enlisted together and started basic long before Bill and Arty. During training, an exploding shell peppered Kirby with shrapnel and he spent two months in the hospital. Shy and quiet, he kept to himself most of the time although he seemed to hit it off with Arty. Of course, everyone got along with Arty.

"I think I might. Give me a minute to get my shirt and shoes on." Arty slid out of his hammock.

"How about you, Zim?" Kirby clung to a pole as the ship rolled.

"Naw, I think I'll pass." Bill didn't know what to say to God anymore than he knew what to say to his mother.

"This won't take long," Arty said and followed Kirby up the aisle towards the top deck.

Smitty, back from visiting with Cordell, climbed into his hammock beside Bill a few minutes later. "I'm nervous as hell about tomorrow. The whole idea of running across a beach with someone shooting at us gives me the willies." Smitty wiggled around trying to get comfortable.

Bill's hammock was second from the top and way over his head. It took several attempts for him to crawl in and get settled. "Not m-me. I like running across beaches when I'm being shot at. It's my favorite thing."

"For crying out loud, will you guys shut up? I'm trying to get some sleep here." The man above Bill growled.

"Barton, don't you ever do anything but complain?" Bill nudged the man's hammock with his toe.

"Goddammit, Zimmer. Am I gonna have to call the Sarge? I got a headache from the nasty smell down here. You'd think the Navy would keep this place cleaner."

Bill lay in the hammock thinking about RL and wondering what it felt like to die. He pretended to be asleep when Arty and Kirby came back, but he was still awake when Smitty grunted and rolled out of his bed in search of the head several hours later.

Chapter 3 -- The Prelude

It was still dark at 4:00 A.M. Bill and Arty stood together in the chow line with hundreds of other somber boys.

"Where the hell is Smitty?" Bill scanned the faces around him. "I haven't seen him since last night."

"Look at that chow." Arty craned his neck. "Steak and eggs. They are doing us up right this morning."

"This is like the last meal they cook up for a prisoner about to be fried," someone behind Bill said.

"Traditional pre-battle breakfast." The server grinned and ladled scrambled eggs onto Bill's plate.

"I don't know if this is so smart." Doc Kline was two Marines down from Arty in the line.

"Why's that, Doc?" Arty peered at the Navy corpsman over his frameless eyeglasses.

"Lot of these guys are gonna have stomach wounds or need surgery in a few hours. All this food is gonna complicate things. I suggest you boys eat light."

"Aw Doc, you are a worrier." Cordell stood in line behind Kline. "This might be the only good meal we have for a few days. After this it's K-rations."

"So what do we do? Eat light or eat hearty?" Arty nudged Bill.

"I'm going to eat hearty." Bill decided as they set their trays down on a long table. "I don't intend to get a stomach wound."

"Me too." Arty pushed his eggs around with his fork. "I can't tell if they are fresh or powdered anymore."

Bill took a bite. "Powdered."

"Mine are runny." Cliff Barton sat down next to Bill. "You'd think the Navy would at least make sure breakfast this morning was prepared right."

"Come on, B-Barton. It's steak and eggs."

"I couldn't sleep a wink last night. I twisted my ankle yesterday afternoon and it's all puffed up. Ached all night. Think I'll go have the corpsman take a look at it." No one liked Barton very much.

Cordell sat down on the other side of Bill and rubbed his palms together. "Today's the day!"

Bill grabbed his hand. "What the hell you g-got there, a bug?"

"This is a genuine carved black coral ring. It's an antique or something. I got it in Honolulu. Big fat guy in a flowered shirt sold it to me. He said it was good luck."

"It's bigger than a marble. You're gonna get it caught on something." Arty examined it with the eye of a professional jeweler.

"I'm not superstitious or anything, but I think having a good luck charm gives you an edge." Cordell flipped them the bird with his ring finger.

"Leave it to a d-damned Yankee to give us the wrong finger." Bill laid down his fork leaving his half eaten steak on the plate.

"I figure my grandkids will get a kick out the ring I wore in battle." Cordell blew on the stone and rubbed it against his sleeve.

"My God, there's Smitty. He looks awful." Arty laid his silverware down too.

"Where you b-been, pal?" Bill moved over and Smitty squeezed in between him and Barton.

"I musta ate something that came back on me. Been in the head since 2:30 this morning." Smitty dug into his eggs. "I bout fell in when they rang that damned gong or whatever it was at 3 A.M."

Cordell swallowed a piece of meat and forked another. "Did you take that stuff I gave you?"

"Not yet."

"Are you okay now?"

"Well, no, but I'm hungry." Smitty chewed with his mouth open. "Can I have what's left of your steak, Zim?"

"Be my guest." Bill wiped the sweat off his upper lip and took a deep breath.

"That's disgusting, Smith." Barton rolled his eyes. "Do you realize how many germs you can get from eating someone else's food?"

• • • • •

It was a clear, beautiful morning. Ringed with glossy black beaches, the pork chop shaped island rose out of the bright blue water. By 6:30, the armada surrounding it was buzzing with activity. Dressed in their battle gear, Bill, Arty, Kirby, Smitty and Cordell went up on deck to watch sailors slinging thick-roped nets over the sides of the troop transports.

"It looks deserted." Arty lit a cigarette.

Kirby leaned against the railing and lit one of his own. "Can't be too many Japs left alive after all the shelling."

Wisps of smoke curled toward the sky here and there so that island seemed to be steaming. Bill thought the whole place was spooky. How hard would anyone fight to protect such a barren piece of nothingness in the middle of nowhere? Maybe they wouldn't. Maybe they'd all be gone by the time the boats hit the beach.

"Is that Suribachi?" Cordell pointed to what looked like a pile of smashed concrete at the narrow end of the island.

"What else could it be?" Kirby narrowed his eyes. "I don't see anything else that could be called a mountain."

Even if the Japs wanted to run away, where could they go, Bill wondered. Underground? Maybe they'd give up when they saw how many Marines were coming after them.

"I hope we don't get separated," Arty said suddenly. "I don't mind dying so much as I hate the idea of dying alone."

Bill looked to Arty to know what to do just as he had with RL. It upset him to hear Arty talking like that, to think about Arty dying. The others fidgeted, shifting from one foot to the other as if they didn't know what to do either.

"We'll stick together. Hell, it'll only be a couple of days." Smitty thumped Arty on the arm. "Besides, you'll outlive all of us."

Loudspeakers blared and Bill jumped. He couldn't get used to life on a ship. For a moment, he was glad that this was the last day. Then he thought about what they were about to do and he wished he could crawl back into his hammock. All around him, sailors went about their tasks. Heavily armed Marines began climbing over the sides of the ships using the thick nets to get to the Higgins boats below them.

As they watched, a man on one of the other ships lost his grip and fell into the ocean. Bill shuddered. "Arty, I'll stay with you. Don't worry. I don't know how m-much I can do -- b-but, I'll stay close. "

"And I'm sticking close to Zim." Cordell elbowed Bill and grinned. "I know from experience about this little guy."

"Aww, cut it out." Bill blushed.

"Let's make a pact that we'll take care of one another." Arty stuck out his hand.

"You g-got it, buddy." Bill put his hand over Arty's.

"I'm in." Cordell put his hand over Bill's.

"Me too." Kirby reached over Bill's head.

"And me." Smitty joined in. "Damn, Cordell. That ring pinched the shit outta me."

"Nag, nag. It'll keep us all safe. It's good luck." When Cordell laughed, everyone else in the group had to smile.

"GANGWAY!" A Marine sergeant bellowed. The boys moved aside as another unit hurried by. Young and determined, they were to be in one of the first waves. "Go get 'em, brother." Kirby slapped one of them on the back. Bill recognized the white-faced young private as one of the guys Kirby knew from back home.

"Good luck, you crazy bastards." Cordell shook a fist in the air.

Bill locked eyes with a Marine he'd played pinochle with back in Hawaii. Neither of them said anything. Bill felt like crying.

At 6:40, the Navy resumed bombarding the island. This close to the action, the noise was deafening. The boys held their hands over their ears and watched as shell after shell arced

116

over their heads and onto the island.

"My God!" Smitty mouthed and Bill nodded his head. Orange flashes and smudgy gray smoke dotted Suribachi and the beaches below it. Smaller gunboats moved closer and launched rockets at various targets on the island.

"Okay, you bastards. Here's some toys for you to play with." Kroner's voice startled them out of their noise-induced reveries. Passing out ammunition and grenades, the Sarge put on a show of good cheer that Bill didn't buy this time. "Take some care with these sonuvabitches. Don't go blowing your gonads off."

Bill turned the live grenades over in his hand as though they were eggs. "This is for real," he said as he hung them on his belt.

"Yeah, I guess we are going to do this." Arty helped Bill heft a forty-pound machine gun onto his back. "I'll never understand why they made a little guy like you a machine gunner."

"I c-can do it."

"I know you can do it. It's just doesn't seem right that you have to is all."

The water around Iwo Jima was crowded. There were close to eight hundred ships moored off the island. Higgins boats and Amtracs filled with Marines waited for the signal to head toward shore. Still more craft snugged up against the troop carriers while thousands more men scrambled down the nets to make up the next wave.

"That must be the Line of Departure." Arty gestured with his head. About two miles offshore, directly in front of them and parallel with the beaches, two control vessels moved into position at either end of an imaginary line. Smaller crafts marked out boat lanes. The boys strained their eyes to make out what was going on.

"B-Bet those guys are getting seasick. They already b-been out there for over an hour." Bill yelled over the noise of the big guns.

"Okay, boys. It's time for us too." Kroner waved his arms to get their attention. "Get your goddamn helmets on and strapped. We are going to crawl over the side of this bastard and get in the Higgins boats just like we practiced before. OKAY? The surf's not too bad right now, but if you fall in, it's not going to be so easy to fish your ass out. SO DON'T FALL IN! Now, we'll probably circle awhile before we go in. When we do go in, you stay close to me. I'll get you through this, understand? STAY CLOSE TO ME!"

Bill planned on doing just that. The Sarge never let him down yet.

Kroner pointed toward the disembarkation area. Arty nodded and led the way. Bill and Kirby shuffled after him, looking back nervously. Cordell shifted his pack, squared his shoulders and followed.

"I'm gonna be sick!" Kendall Smith cried.

"Get your ass on down there, Smitty."

"But Sarge, I'm going to puke."

"Puke over the side and make it snappy."

"I gotta take a crap," Smitty pleaded.

"It's too late, Smitty. You're going to have to deal with it."

Kendall Smith leaned over the side and heaved up his breakfast.

Bill focused on the back of Arty's head, trying not to think about what was happening to Smitty or what was about to happen when they reached the beach. One by one, they climbed over the edge of the ship and down the side net. They had practiced it so many times before that everything went off without a hitch.

"NOW, Smith!" Kroner ordered as Cordell dropped into the bottom of the boat.

Smitty wiped his mouth on the back of his sleeve and staggered to the disembarkation area a few feet away. He looked down into the boat below where the other boys stared up at him. He was pale and sweating, but he threw his leg over the side. Half way down the net, he clung to the ropes and vomited again, soiling the front of his shirt.

"Shit, man. Get OVER it, will you? This damned boat stinks enough as it is." A whiny voice complained from below.

"You leave him the hell alone!" Arty wheeled on Cliff Barton, his face contorted with fury.

Bill had never seen Arty yell at anyone before. He backed against the side of the boat, not quite knowing what he should do.

Barton blanched but stood his ground. "I don't think I'm going to make it to shore without being sick and it's that bastard's fault." He pointed at Smitty clinging to the nets above them.

"He shoulda taken the powder I gave him." Cordell started back up the net to help Smitty.

"CORDELL! GET BACK IN THAT BOAT BEFORE I COME DOWN THERE AND CRAWL DOWN YOUR THROAT."

"Aw, Sarge. He's sick."

"CORDELL!"

Cordell let go of the ropes and elbowed his way past Barton, who turned around and gave Bill a push.

"Hey," Bill jerked away. "Cut it out."

Kroner climbed down the side of the ship and grabbed Smitty by the neck of his uniform. "You are holding us up. GET DOWN THERE NOW! Otherwise I'm throwing your ass in the fucking ocean."

Smitty looked over his shoulder. The gap between the ship and the Higgins boat opened and closed with the surf.

"Come on, buddy. You can do it," Arty called.

"Asshole like that is going to get someone killed."

Cordell clenched his fist. "One more word and I'll punch your lights out, Barton."

Smitty closed his eyes, jumped into the boat and slumped to the floor. Arty knelt to check on him. Hoping Smitty hadn't broken anything, Bill looked around for Doc Kline. Apparently, he'd been assigned to a different boat. What if they needed him? Damn Navy.

Kroner was the last aboard. They pushed off from the troop ship a little after 8:00 A.M. The seaman found his position and began circling. The engine was a continuous roar. Thirty-two men stood in the boat, trying to keep their balance. Exhaust fumes and the smell of vomit choked them. Three Marines, including Barton, gagged as the boat hit choppy water.

The battleships kept pounding the island. The boys squinted to see through the smoke as they circled. Then the firing stopped.

"What's happening now?" Kirby's voice broke the sudden silence.

A distant buzzing grew louder. Bill covered his eyes and

squinted into the sun. Carrier planes flew over them and attacked the island.

"Those are Navy planes." Smitty forgot about being sick and perked up. "Go get 'em NAVY!"

Cordell punched his left fist into the air as plane after plane swooped in, dropping fiery napalm bombs and strafing the beach.

Cheers came from hundreds of other ships and boats around them.

"Here come the Marines!" Arty pounded Bill on the back. As the Navy planes headed back to their carriers, forty-eight gull-wing fighters bore down on the smoking island. The cheering from the boats grew louder as Marine Pilots took over the task of further softening up the enemy. The sun shone brightly.

"They ain't gonna leave any Japs for us!" Cordell pretended to pout. Bill hoped they were all good and dead. He wouldn't miss them at all.

As the last plane headed back to its ship, the naval shelling began once again. The boys shuffled around the boat with grim excitement. The noise and activity around them filled the air with an electric charge.

At 8:15, the first three waves of troops and equipment posed at the Line of Departure waiting for the signal to go in. Eight more waves circled behind them, ready to land at five-minute intervals. At 8:57, the shelling stopped.

"There they go," Kirby shouted as the first three waves headed toward the landing area under Suribachi. The noise of the boat's engine made it hard to converse. Hearing fire from shore, Bill and Arty looked over their shoulders as they circled. It didn't seem too bad, certainly not like Bill had expected. The

Marines continued landing in waves. Each time the boat came around, there was more and more heavy equipment piled up on the distant beach.

"Why aren't they clearing that stuff off the beach?" Kroner yelled to the seaman running the Higgins boat. "It's turning into a frigging trash heap. How are we going to get these boys in there?"

The young man shrugged.

"When do you think we're going in?" Bill turned to Arty.

"Don't know, buddy. How long have we been out here?"

Bill held up two fingers. "Two hours!"

The noise from shore increased. The boys watched in horror as enemy machine guns, mortars and heavy artillery raked the beaches. The Japanese had held their fire until thousands of Marines landed. Now, two hours after the beginning of the invasion, they concentrated all their resources on destroying the men and equipment piled up on the beaches.

Kroner stared at the shoreline, turning to keep it in sight as the Higgins boat circled.

"You think Kroner's worried?" Bill cupped his hand over Smitty's ear.

"I don't know, but I'm ready to get out of this friggin boat. My stomach's giving me hell."

"Try not to think about it." Bill wondered why Kroner didn't send Smitty back to sickbay. There were thousands of them out here on the water. What difference did one sick kid make?

The sun bore down on them. Round and round they went. Bill began to daydream about that pretty black-eyed girl who lived at the bottom of Bailey Hill back in Fort Smith. Ioké had black eyes too. That was the first thing he noticed about her when they met at Jimmy's in Hilo. He wondered if either of them would remember him.

"OKAY. HERE WE GO." Kroner shouted at 11:00 A.M.

Bill gripped his weapon, his heart pounding in his chest. He was ready. They motored out of the circling pattern and headed for the Line of Departure. As they approached, he could see boats turning around and heading back toward the holding area.

"What the fuck's going on now?" Kroner threw his helmet on the floor. Bill danced away to avoid being hit. The boys looked at each other in confusion as the seaman turned their boat around as well. Maybe the first waves already took the island. Maybe they weren't even going to land. Maybe they could go home now.

More circling. Bill yawned. After forty minutes, Smitty and Cordell dozed, their helmeted heads resting on their chests as they leaned against the side of the Higgins Boat.

Bill edged closer to Arty. "What do you think that was?"

"False alarm, I guess. Sure pissed Kroner off whatever it was."

"This waiting is getting to m-me. Look at those g-guys, I can't b-believe they c-can sleep through this."

"I hope no one I know died this morning."

Arty's blunt words stunned Bill. He thought about the young pinochle player and Kirby's friend. They were probably already on that beach. He peered over the side of the boat as they came round toward the island. "Looks like a lot of junk on the b-beach and there's some kind of m-movement. Kinda like teensy ants. M-must be the m-men, m-maybe jeeps and shit. Lotta firing, b-but can't tell if it's them or us."

"I wonder what it's like on those beaches." Arty tightened the lid of his canteen, checked his grenades, felt for his wallet in his back pocket.

"Can't be too m-much different than what we practiced on Hilo." Bill followed Arty's example and started checking his gear too. It was something to do. It was better than thinking about Marines dying on the beach.

Pretty soon other boys were rummaging through their packs as well. Barton elbowed his way to the side of the boat and slipped his arms out of his pack.

"I wouldn't do that if I were you," Arty said. "Kroner will have a fit."

"Sarge can stick it up his ass." Barton dug into his pack just as the boat hit a big wave. It fell to the floor and tipped over dumping out the contents. The boys nearby stared at the cornucopia lying at their feet. Something silver glinted in the sunshine.

Arty's mouth dropped open. "My mezuzah!"

"There's my Zippo." Another boy pointed. "I thought I lost it."

Bill narrowed his eyes. "You lousy sonofa-b-bitch. You're the thief."

"Look, Barton's got that medal Lieberman's been looking for." Kirby elbowed Cordell.

Cordell pushed his helmet back from his forehead. Scowling, he poked Smitty who startled awake.

Smitty rubbed his eyes and then focused on the collection of stolen items lying on the floor of the boat. "That bastard has Aunt Gert's taffy."

Cornered, Barton glanced over the angry faces around him

124

looking for Kroner who was at the front of the boat focused on the beach. "This is my stuff. Keep your hands off."

Bill stepped forward bristling with indignation. "You have a f-fucking Jewish medal?"

"I bought it off a fellow in Hawaii."

"You stole it."

Barton knelt down to gather up his goods. "Back off, asshole."

"G-give that medal b-back." Bill grabbed Barton's shirtsleeve.

"You ain't gonna do nothing but stand there and stutter, you little piss ant!" Barton jerked his arm away.

Bill roared and charged, knocking Barton on his butt in the bottom of the boat.

"HEY, HEY, HEY. Save that for the Japs." Kroner pushed his way through the boys crowded around Bill and Cliff Barton.

"He was giving me the business, Sarge. Just cause I'm not feeling well, he crawled up my ass."

"SHUT THE FUCK UP, BARTON." Kroner's face was bright red and the veins in his neck stood out. Barton backed away and pouted. Bill exchanged hateful glances with him.

"I can't believe you girls. Wasting energy on shit like this! We are about to take a hot beach and you are getting into fistfights in the landing boat? Fighting each OTHER? We are brothers. We gotta take care of each other here."

"It wasn't MY fault, Sarge. Zim started it," Barton whined.

"That's not true. Barton was giving Smitty a hard time and Zimmer took up for him." Arty stepped forward.

125

"That's right." Kirby joined in.

"WILL YOU LADIES CAN IT? Act like Marines or I'm gonna toss the lot of you into the ocean." Kroner glowered at them under his thick brows.

They watched Barton gather up their belongings from the bottom of the boat.

"Fine. It won't be much longer now." Kroner went back to the front of the boat.

Barton stood up and handed the mezuzah to Arty. "Why didn't you tell the Sarge?"

"It wasn't the right time or place."

Bill still wanted to hit him. "We'll d-deal with you later after all this is over."

"Yeah, ya will." Barton dropped the bag of taffy into Smitty's hand before squeezing through the ring of Marines and settling in at the back of the boat.

"God-d-damned snake."

Arty stared at the elaborate silver pendant in his hand. "My mother gave me this."

"Glad it finally turned up." Smitty clapped Arty on the back. "Damn, I'm hungry."

"I guess I was feeling superstitious." Arty took off his helmet and slipped the chain over his head, tucking the mezuzah in under his t-shirt with his dog tags.

"We all are, buddy. Look at Cordell and his ring." Smitty chuckled as he munched on the candy Barton had returned to him.

"I wouldn't have wanted to go in without this." Kirby pulled the crucifix he wore out of his collar."

"Hey, b-buddy. Whatever works." Bill shrugged. None of it made much sense to him. He and RL only went to church when someone got married or buried. Their grandmother was half Cherokee and a big believer though. Maybe she was praying for him now. Of course, she probably prayed for RL too. Fat lot of good that did.

"I thought for sure we'd have been on the beach by now." Kirby tucked the cross back inside his shirt.

"Why did they t-turn us around?"

"Kroner said the beach was closed, that's all I know." Kirby turned his back to the wind and lit a cigarette.

"You gonna be able to keep that down?" Arty raised an eyebrow at Smitty who was on his second piece of taffy.

"Oh hell, yes. I'm okay now. Stomach's settled." "Nothing like something sweet to get the taste of puke outta your mouth."

"You amaze me, Smith." Arty chuckled.

"Just don't start up-chucking again, pal. Or I'll join you this time." Kirby's smoke rings drifted away on the wind.

Bill felt great. He'd been alone since RL died. Now he had friends who would support him when he needed them even if it was over an asshole like Cliff Barton. He wasn't just RL's little brother anymore. He was a Marine. His country was counting on him. His friends were counting on him. He stood a little straighter, promising himself that he wouldn't let Arty or Kirby or Smitty or Cordell or the Sarge down. Barton could go fuck himself.

Chapter 4 -- The Beach

Two hours later, they started for shore. This time when they approached the Line of Departure, they were given the signal to go in. The waves slammed into the boats as they accelerated towards the island.

"REMEMBER WHAT I SAID, MEN. STAY WITH ME. WHERE I GO, YOU GO," Kroner shouted, as the roar of the Japanese guns grew louder. "YOU STAY WITH ME, YOU ARE GOING TO BE OKAY. YOU WANDER OFF BY YOURSELF AND YOU'RE GONNA GET YOUR ASSES CREAMED."

Gasping as the wind blew in his face, Bill gripped his rifle. Stay with Kroner. That's all he had to remember. Stay with Kroner.

It was approaching 3:00 P.M. as they neared the beach with dozens of other boats.

"Good luck." Arty mouthed to Bill. Bill nodded, his jaws locked and he gritted his teeth. He looked around for Smitty and Cordell. Smitty was right behind him. Cordell was a few paces back shifting his pack. He gave Bill a thumbs up and grinned. Bill turned forward just as a huge explosion shook the vessel. He fell into the bottom of the boat, cracking his elbow. A shell landed in the water only a few yards away drenching everyone with cold water. Bill struggled to one knee. The craft hit the beach with a thud and he fell back onto the floor again.

"Get up, pal. Get up." Arty tried to help Bill to his feet. The noise from shells and mortars was deafening. Machine gun rapid fire sounded like a woodpecker pecking at the boat – tap, tap, tap! They recognized small arms fire amidst the din. The front of the boat dropped open forming a ramp onto the beach.

The boys spilled out yelling. A bullet whizzed by Bill's ear and hit the boy next to him in the mouth. Bill turned to see the frozen look of horror on the young Marine's face as he fell. Bill stepped over the body and ran out onto the beach, his feet sinking into the black sand. He looked left and right. Where was Arty? He'd lost Arty.

The beach was littered with equipment and body parts. He froze. A long trail of wet, glistening intestines lay in front of him. He turned to the right, a torso floated in the surf a few feet away. The boys behind him pushed forward. He couldn't find Arty. A bullet tore through his right sleeve, but didn't touch him. He saw Kroner several yards ahead of him. He started running, vaguely aware of a high, howling sound that rose over the din of battle. Then he realized it was his own voice and that he was crying.

He could see Kroner but he couldn't get to him. Kirby sprinted past him like a deer holding his rifle in both hands. Bill felt like he was running in syrup. The black sand was about the size of rock salt and so deep that he sank to his knees in places. His heart pounded with the exertion. He had to get to Kroner. Arty would be with Kroner. He'd be okay if he stayed with Kroner.

Kroner exploded.

Small bits of flesh splattered Bill's face and then he was hit in the chest so hard that he fell over backwards. He lay there for a moment, dazed. He tried to roll over onto his belly but he couldn't. The machine gun was strapped to his back as well as ammunition and the fully loaded pack. He was like a beetle, his arms and legs churning in the air, trying to get the leverage to turn over.

Someone fell beside him. It was Barton. He gave Bill a push and suddenly Bill was on his stomach. He opened his eyes and saw what had knocked him down. It was Kroner's head. It lay

129

a few feet away, the face frozen in an open mouthed scream. Barton saw it at the same time Bill did. His eyes bulged and he shrieked in horror -- over and over again. Bill screamed with him. They lay there on the beach together screaming until nothing came out anymore. Barton clambered to his feet and ran off down the beach.

Bill's left hand was stinging. A small sliver of bone pierced the skin, but there was no blood. He wondered if he was hurt. He touched it with his finger. It wasn't HIS bone. It must have been Kroner's. He closed his eyes and pulled it out of his hand. He didn't know what to do with it, so he put it in his pocket.

He was aware of more explosions. Bullets were everywhere. He was supposed to stay with Kroner. NOW what was he supposed to do? He didn't see anyone he knew. There were Marines lying on their bellies all around him, their faces pressed into the sand. He couldn't tell if they were alive or dead. No one was moving. He could hear machine gun fire. Sometimes the bullets slammed into the sand around him. Bigger explosions tossed men and body parts into the air. He was alone on the crowded beach. Exhausted, he slept.

He opened his eyes a few minutes later. He was cold. A flash and a loud noise, then searing heat washed over him. Something lifted him a few inches from the ground and then threw him down again. Grit was in his eyes. He rubbed them. Tried to see. Rubbed them again. The concussion had thrown him a foot or so closer to Kroner's head. Kroner still wore his helmet strapped tightly under his chin. His black eyes glittered under their bushy brows. Bill could see a silver filling in one of Kroner's teeth. Funny he'd never noticed it before.

Something flashed beyond Kroner. Bill couldn't quite make out what it was. It glowed like gold sometimes, other times it seemed black. What WAS it? He inched forward. A bullet plowed into the sand near his foot. He wiggled frantically and moved forward about three feet. Here the sand wasn't so wet. It was warmer. He squinted. He still couldn't see what it was. He inched up a little slope, a terrace. Black sand fell down on him as he struggled. What WAS it?

He lay on his stomach and stared at the object. It was an arm, torn from its owner near the shoulder. Dark blood caked the sleeve. The hand lay palm down, the nails had grit under them -- and there was a carved black coral ring about the size of a marble on the ring finger.

Bill had no wind. Just like that, the first minute on the beach. No chance. He turned his head and puked sour-tasting water into the sand beside him. His stomach was empty. It was 4:00 P.M. He had eaten nothing for twelve hours.

Someone grabbed his foot. He screamed in terror as he felt himself being dragged backwards, his fingers plowing tracks in the sand. Machine gun fire sprayed around him. He expected its sting at any moment.

"ZIM! It's ME!" Arty whispered as he pulled Bill into a shallow shell hole. Sand fell in around them and they plastered themselves flat, waiting for the machine gun fire to move on.

"Arty!" Bill cried. "I lost you, pal. Where did you go?"

"I was with Kroner. I was right with him -- and Cordell."

"When I left the b-boat, Cordell was b-behind me. How did he get here?"

"We were all with Kroner, Zim."

"Where's Smitty?"

"I don't know, I don't know." Arty's glasses were coated with sand and blood and bits of flesh.

"You know that b-boy from Florida who used to talk about alligators in his b-back yard?"

131

"Fred Hurley?"

"Yeah, Fred. He got it in the b-boat. As soon as that fucking front panel went down, a b-bullet went right in his m-mouth. Damnedest thing I ever saw. Went right in his m-mouth, for crying out loud." Bill's voice broke. An explosion killed a man a few feet away. They ducked down and shuddered as the warm spray of blood hit their faces.

"We need to get OUT of here, b-buddy." Bill's throat was raw. "They are going to get us here."

"Where should we go?" Arty took off his glasses, wiped the lenses with his thumb and then put them back on. "There's no safe place. We can't go back towards the boats, it's worse there. I know we are supposed to go forward, but I'm all turned around. Which way IS forward?"

"Did you see what h-happened to Kroner?" Tears ran down Bill's face. He wiped his nose with the back of his sleeve.

"I think he's married. I think he's got a kid."

"His head h-hit me in the chest, Arty. It knocked me flat on my b-back."

"SHIT!" Arty ducked as more bullets zinged over his head.

"I think Cordell's dead too." Bill pressed his face into the sand, holding his hands over his helmet. "His arm is over there."

"I was with him, Zim."

"Talk about luck. We hadn't b-been on the damned b-beach m-more than a m-minute. I couldn't have been m-more than ten feet b-behind you all."

"The same shell that got Kroner got Cordell and two other guys too." Arty flinched as someone ran past the shell hole. "I don't know what happened to Kirby or Smitty. I haven't seen them since we left the boat."

"I can't b-believe Cordell's dead. We had b-breakfast with him this m-morning." Bill's teeth chattered. "He couldn't have taken m-more than ten steps on the b-beach."

"Doc Kline gave him a shot right away, but he was screaming, Zim. He was squirming around and screaming. We couldn't get him off the beach because they were still shooting at us. He bled to death right in front of us. Doc had to move on to help some other guy."

"Where is he?"

"He's only a few feet from Kroner."

"M-maybe we ought to get b-both of them b-back to the b-boats. We c-can't just leave them there."

Another explosion threw sand over them.

"How we gonna do that? We can't even move."

"We should do SOMETHING. We shouldn't leave them there to b-be b-blown up again and again." Bill couldn't think -- if things would just settle down for a moment, then he could figure out what they should do.

"All right, men. Let's move forward." An officer crawled forward and paused beside them.

"Where are we going, sir?" Arty asked.

"That way." The officer pointed.

"What about our friends b-back there?"

"They'll be taken care of, son. Your job is to move forward." The man lunged forward and then slid backwards in the deep sand. Progress was slow. Bill and Arty followed.

Chapter 5 -- The First Night

Bill and Arty huddled together in a poorly dug foxhole. They were just beyond the beach somewhere between Suribachi and a Japanese airfield. They were cold even though they both wore their ponchos.

"Should we set up the m-machine gun?"

"Who we gonna shoot at?" They couldn't see much in the blackness, but they could sense movement about them. Neither of them knew what they were supposed to do now but hide.

Bill was furious. Kroner had told them he'd take care of them. He said they'd be safe. How could the sonuvabitch go and get killed that way? Bill rubbed the heel of his hand over his sternum. It was sore where Kroner's head hit him. "I heard stories about Japs coming b-back at you after dark. What do they call them? B-Banjo charges?"

"Banzai Charges." Arty swiveled his head left and right, alert for any noise.

Mortars and shells crashed into the area behind them, shrapnel and debris spewing in all directions. They pressed themselves deep into the hole, their arms covering their helmets. Silence.

"We ain't even SEEN a Jap yet." The hairs on the back of Bill's neck rose and he spun in a small circle, his heels burrowing into the hard packed gravel in the bottom of the hole.

"I know they are out there. I can feel them in the dark." Arty peered over the lip of the hole. "I wonder where Smitty is." He ducked to avoid an imaginary bullet.

There was a loud pop. A flare lit the battlefield while it floated to earth on a little parachute. There was sporadic firing all around them. Unable to tell who was shooting at whom, they crouched low in the foxhole afraid a stray bullet would find them. Then blackness covered them again.

Something moved under their feet making scratchy, scraping sounds. They cried out. Bill lifted first one leg and then the other, shuddering and cursing. Arty stabbed at it with his bayonet. Holding up his rifle barrel, they saw that it was a land crab. Disgusted, he flipped it out.

Someone yelled and stamped a few feet away as the crab landed in another hole.

"Hey, there's someone over there."

"Shh, we d-don't want to b-bring the whole Jap army d-down on us."

"You think the Japs don't know we're here? What if it's someone we know and they need help?"

Bill thought about what it would be like to be out there alone. "Okay."

Arty straightened up. "WHO'S OVER THERE?"

"It's me. Danny Kline."

"Danny Kline?"

"You know me, Lieberman. I'm the corpsman for this unit."

"D-DOC?" Bill's head popped up.

"Who's with you, Lieberman?"

"Zimmer."

"Are you both okay?"

"We're okay."

"Do you guys have room for me over there?"

Bill was relieved when Arty answered. "It's close with two. Might be tight with three."

"Okay." Doc Kline's voice sounded funny. Strained.

"W-what's wrong, D-Doc?"

"Captain Reese is here with me. He's been dead for awhile now."

Arty turned to Bill and raised an eyebrow. Bill couldn't imagine spending the night with a corpse. That was worse than being alone in the dark. "We'll m-make room, Doc."

"Okay. I'm coming over."

A noise from the opposite direction startled them.

"WHAT'S THAT?" Bill ducked down deeper in the hole, panting.

A line of shadows passed behind their foxhole, maybe ten yards away. There was whispering in a foreign language. The voices were high pitched and young. Bill and Arty cowered, hearts pounding, praying that the Japanese didn't see them or Doc. The enemy footsteps receded.

They waited in silence for several minutes.

Arty rose up again. "Doc?"

"Yeah?"

"You want to come over now?"

"I think I'll just stay here."

"Are you sure?"

"I was out in the open when they went by. All they had to do was look my way."

"Come on, Doc. They're gone now."

"I-I don't think I can make myself."

Bill didn't think he could scurry across those few feet of open space either. "That's okay, b-buddy. W-we're here if you n-need us."

"Thanks anyway, fellas."

"We'll see you in the morning, Doc."

"Get some rest. Who knows what it's going to be like tomorrow." Doc's voice quivered as he settled in to sleep beside Captain Reese.

Bill was exhausted but he couldn't stop thinking about Captain Reese and Cordell and the Pinochle boy -- and Kroner. "You go ahead and take a nap, Arty."

"Naw, Zim. I'm wide awake."

Somewhere in the night, someone was crying. Gunshots -- first small arms fire, then bigger ordinance.

"Did Cordell know he was d-dying?"

"He knew. I shoulda done something for him. He was hurting and I shoulda done something for him. I just didn't have the guts."

"You were w-with him. You stayed with him. There w-wasn't anything else you could do." Something fluttered over their heads. Bill spun around, eyes wide -- gripping his rifle. A bat.

They both sighed with relief.

"Cordell was hurting. He was dying and he was scared. I shoulda put him out of his misery." Arty bowed his head as though praying.

"You mean k-kill him?" Bill was aghast.

"He was in agony, Zim. I wouldn't be able to stand that kind of pain. He was crying for his momma. He begged me to shoot him. I didn't have the guts. I let him down." Arty put both hands over his face and cried, his shoulders shaking.

"It's – it's okay, buddy." Bill started to pat Arty on the shoulder, withdrew his hand -- tried again. Arty took a deep breath and wiped his nose with his sleeve. Relieved that Arty seemed to be better, Bill stuck his hand in his pocket.

"Zim?"

"Yeah?"

"I'm glad we are together. I feel better knowing you are there."

"Why?"

"You are stronger than the rest of us."

"What?" Bill recoiled in surprise. He was the perennial little brother -- the fuck-up, the little guy that no one took seriously.

"Smitty and Cordell told us about what happened in Hilo Bay. Look how you stood up to Barton today. We all count on you, Zim. You're the one with the guts."

Bill shuddered. He was a scared little boy -- just as he'd always been but if he kept real quiet, maybe no one else would notice. "I ain't even shot this thing yet." Bill wiped wet sand off his rifle. The machine gun was still strapped to his back. "I don't know if I can."

"We haven't had anything to shoot at. We've just been trying to avoid being shot ourselves." Arty took off his glasses and rubbed his eyes.

"Did Cordell say anything?" Bill asked after a minute. His horror of wounds had turned to fascination.

"Not much. His arm and leg was off, and he had an awful stomach wound." Arty closed his eyes. "I never saw anyone hurt like that before."

"He ate hearty." Bill remembered.

"Was that only this morning?"

"They are still there, you know. Cordell and Kroner are still on the b-beach." Bill stared out towards the ocean.

"Poor bastards. The crabs are probably chewing on them." Arty glanced seaward too and shuddered. The surf pounded against the beach.

Chapter 6 -- The Second Day

By dawn the weather had turned sour. The wind was cold to men trained in Hawaii. Dark clouds threatened rain, but there was enough visibility for carrier planes to attack Suribachi. They swooped and strafed and dropped napalm. Bill and Arty watched in horror from their position not far from the base of the tiny mountain. Planes dove so low they could see the grim faces of the young pilots.

"Sounds a lot different HERE than it did out in that damned boat." Arty held his hands over his ears.

"Look at the b-beach." Bill stared at the stinking, body-littered beach a few yards away. "They were alive yesterday."

"Where's Doc?"

"There was someone c-calling for help just before dawn. I g-guess he w-went to t-take care of them."

"Does anyone look familiar? I don't know what we are supposed to do." Arty peeked left and right, his teeth chattering. "I think we are lost."

"How can we b-be lost? There's the m-mountain b-behind us. We just need to find our group. They can't b-be that far away. We all went the same direction when we got off the b-boat." A fine spray of cold rain caused Bill to shiver.

"Is that Barton over there? I never thought I'd be glad to see THAT slimy bastard."

"And there's K-Kirby." Bill was relieved to see a flash of red hair as a tall Marine a few yards away repositioned his helmet. "We just do what they do until we g-get orders to d-do something else."

"We must be moving forward." Dozens of men in foxholes and shell holes begin to emerge. Lying flat on the ground, they inched forward. A machine gun from a pillbox hidden a few yards away forced them back into their hiding places.

"I thought they knocked that bastard out last night." Bill recognized Kirby's voice over the hubbub.

"How'd they get back in there? We DID take that thing last night. The line's already beyond it." A voice behind them answered.

Arty and Bill watched as two men zigzagged in front of the Japanese gunner. Two others approached the pillbox from the side. One of the men went down, screaming in pain and terror. The man on the left side tossed in a grenade. The pillbox exploded. The man on the right unleashed a roaring stream of fire into the small enclosure. They heard shrieks as the gunner was roasted. A disgusting stench reached their nostrils, but they no longer had the urge to heave.

"Die you fucking animal!" Bill yelled. It was the first enemy they could pinpoint. He wanted him dead.

Chapter 7 -- The Long Haul

Smitty and two replacements found them mid-morning several days later.

"You look older," Smitty said to Bill.

Bill was squatted down eating a chocolate bar. He had dropped it in the dirt, but he rinsed it off with his canteen and it was almost good as new. "This is as old as it gets." He finished his candy, and stood up, shouldering his rifle. Dirt caked in his laugh lines. His face was as hairless as a girl's, but his mouth turned downward in a tight grimace.

"What happened to you?" Arty leaned against a rock eating his K-ration for the day.

"I got hit. Right on the friggin beach. Turned around and went back to get treated on the ship."

"So what the hell are you DOING here?" Bill lit a cigarette and drew deeply on it. He was smoking almost as much as Kirby now. Now that he thought about it, so was Arty.

"Well, it wasn't THAT bad and I missed you guys. I mean we were all going to stick together, right?"

"That's a h-hell of a note. You get a chance to g-get out of this shit and you come B-BACK? I can't handle that." Bill scowled and stared off into the distance.

"Well, I'm glad to see you," Arty said. "Where'd they get you?"

"Got a little piece of shrapnel in my butt would you believe? The doc pulled it out with tweezers and gave me a shot. I lay on my belly for a couple of days. Then they sent me out here to find you guys."

"How's your stomach?"

"I took that powdered shit Cordell gave me and I've been fine ever since. Where is that gap-toothed bastard, anyway?" Smitty looked around.

"He's dead." Arty's voice was matter-of-fact, but his eyes twitched.

"Like hell you say!" Smitty dropped his cigarette and took a step back, his mouth open.

"Goddamned Japs b-blew the shit out of him on the b-beach," Bill said. "Kroner too."

"Nooooo." Smitty bent over and took deep breaths.

"You gonna puke?"

"I-I know Cordell's sister, Margie. He fixed me up with her last time we were on leave in San Diego. She's a big, tall blond. Kinda cute. Looked like Cordell. Oh God, what am I gonna tell Margie?"

"I don't think she would want to hear much about it." Arty took another bite and chewed slowly, his chin quivering. "It was pretty ugly."

"What about Cordell's Mom?" Tears ran down Smitty's face.

A husky, dark-skinned boy lay a few feet away talking into a radio. The radio blasted back static and a series of unintelligible sentences ending with "SURIBACHI". Smitty cocked his head and raised his eyebrows.

"Navajo." Arty informed him.

143

"Look." The radioman pointed back at Suribachi. The Stars and Stripes flapped in the wind on top of the mountain. A sudden cheer went up across the island. The ships offshore blasted their horns and shot off their big guns in salute.

"My God. We took that d-damned m-mountain." Bill took a step forward.

"Is it over?" Kirby turned, protecting his pale eyes and freckled face with his hand. "Is it over? Can we go home?"

"WE DID IT!!! Those bastards did it. DAMNED MARINES!" Arty shouted in jubilation.

The two new Marines who came in with Smitty stood up and cheered too. Their faces and uniforms were clean. A sniper shot the smaller one through the neck. He dropped like a rock.

"CORPSMAN! Over here. OVER HERE!" Bill ran to the boy and put his hand over the hole in his throat. Blood spilled through his fingers each time the boy's heart pumped. His eyes were open and his lips were gray.

"NO, NO, NO, NO." Bill sobbed. "Don't do this. You hear m-me. Don't you do this to m-me."

Shells and mortars began crashing down among them. Smitty and Arty dove behind a boulder. The noise was deafening. The sniper continued to fire, little puffs of dirt flying around Bill and the wounded boy. A machine gun twenty yards away sprayed bullets their direction.

"The rest of you get down." Kirby flattened himself on the ground.

"CORPSMAN! CORPSMAN!" Bill cried as the boy's eyes rolled back in his head.

"I'm coming. Give me cover." Doc Kline called from fifty feet away.

144

Kirby aimed in the general direction of the sniper and pulled the trigger. Doc sprinted across a small clearing. The sniper fired shot after shot at him. He knelt on the other side of the wounded boy. Bullets zinged around them.

"There's nothing I can do, Zim. This man is dead."

"Damned f-fucking kid. He wasn't even here l-long enough for me to learn his n-name."

"Calm down. No sense you losing your edge and getting shot too."

Bill let go of the boy's throat and sat back on his heels.

"Come on, pal. Let's get this poor kid out of here." Doc Kline grabbed the dead boy's arms and Bill took his legs. While Arty, Smitty and Kirby kept the sniper busy, Bill and Doc Kline hid the young Marine behind the rock where everyone else was cowering.

"CORPSMAN!"

"I can't do anymore here, Zim." Doc put his hand on Bill's shoulder.

Bill pulled away, his eyes on the wound in the dead boy's throat.

"CORPSMAN!"

"I have to go."

"G-GO, D-DAMNIT!"

Doc straightened his helmet and took off to answer the call. Bill wiped his bloody hands on the dead boy's crisp, clean uniform.

"You all right, Zim?" Arty called from his position behind a small bush.

"Right as r-rain." Bill peered around the rock. The sniper

fired again knocking a chip out of the stone just over Bill's head. "Sonuvabitch!"

The morning wore on. Eventually, the sniper turned his attention elsewhere and they relaxed.

"His name was Stewart. Stewart Bronson. He was from Seattle." Smitty leaned back on the rock, tucking his pants into his crisp new leggings.

"Never knew anyone from Seattle b-before." Bill drank from his canteen and then poured a bit over his hands. Bloody mud dripped from his fingers. The sniper shot three rounds at him. He flipped his invisible tormentor the bird, his face contorted with rage. "I HATE the smell of b-blood."

"His uniform was too clean. They know new guys have clean uniforms. Easy pickin's." Kirby threw a handful of sand at Smitty. Stunned, Smitty glanced over his shoulder in the direction of the sniper.

"My name's Mike Grogan," the remaining replacement said as he poured water over his clothes and rolled in the dirt. "I'm from Clarksburg, West Virginia."

"LET'S GO!" Their new sergeant yelled.

Bill rolled his eyes. Kroner's replacement was just another piss-ant corporal when they hit the beach. If Kroner with all of his experience couldn't protect them, how could this kid?

A figure a few yards away stood up and moved towards a cluster of dark boulders. A second man followed. Kirby and Arty advanced forward, holding their rifles waist level. Smitty scuttled along behind them, keeping his head down.

"Are we just going to leave Stu here?" Grogan stared at his dead friend. Strange-looking beetles had already found the throat wound.

Kirby and Arty disappeared over a little rise in the land ten yards away. Smitty followed a few seconds later. Bill and Grogan looked at each other.

"I ain't staying here by myself," Grogan said.

Bill took a deep breath and nodded. Together, they dashed over the rise to find Smitty, Arty and Kirby crouched over the body of a dead Japanese soldier. The man lay stretched out on his back. His face was peaceful. His lips were full, his dark eyes staring upwards. He was thin and very young. There was a small bullet hole in his right temple. A pistol was still in his right hand. A flat-bladed sword lay by his feet.

"The bastard must have shot himself." Kirby knelt down and stared at the body. Maggots had already begun their work. He lit a cigarette to mask the smell.

"My God, Zim. He looks just like you!" Arty gasped.

"He DOES. He doesn't look Japanese at all. He looks like you." Smitty backed away with a look of revulsion on his face.

Bill stared at the body. "He's dead. I'm not." He picked up the sword and tucked it onto his pack. Smitty pried the pistol out of the corpse's stiff hand and stuck it into the back of his pants.

Chapter 8 -- Smitty

The Marines won the island in inches. Several days later, the boys were still pinned down in a large shell hole only a few yards from the corpse of the Japanese soldier. A machine gun in a cave ahead of them sprayed fire their direction. They ducked their heads below the edge of the hole.

"Wish they'd get that sonuvabitch. We've been laying here for over two hours now." Smitty squirmed. "I gotta go bad."

"You ain't going to go puking on us again are you?" Almost as skinny as Bill now, Kirby didn't ever puke because he didn't eat.

"Naw, I just gotta take a crap. We've been here for hours."

"Damn, Smitty. Your goddamned stomach is going to get us all killed one of these days," Bill said over his shoulder.

"Wish I had more of Cordell's wonder drug. That shit really helped." Smitty grimaced and rubbed his stomach.

"Did I ever tell you about the time Cordell and I went to a fortune teller over in Honolulu?" Arty struggled to find a comfortable position. He was at least fourteen inches taller than Bill and Bill barely had room to move.

"What did the old hag say?" Grogan had become the unit straight man.

"How'd you know she was an old hag?" Arty raised an eyebrow.

"You gotta be an old hag if you are going to tell fortunes. Where you been all your life, Lieberman?" Grogan ducked as bullets kicked up dust around their heads.

"Well, this one was good looking. Dark hair down to her ass, flower at her temple. Black eyes to die for." Arty sighed and patted his chest with his fingertips.

Bill snorted. He'd heard this story a hundred times.

"How good could she be then? She's gotta put on eighty pounds and lose some teeth to qualify." Grogan chuckled.

"Well, anyway, what did the slut say?" Smitty gritted his teeth and rolled on his side.

"She told me I was going to change someone's life. That something I would do would start a chain of events that would change someone's life."

"What the hell d-does THAT mean, Arty?" Sometimes Bill couldn't tell the difference between religious people and superstitious ones.

"I dunno. I asked just that question. She said that was my fate. I would be a trigger."

"A WHAT?" Even Kirby was getting a kick out of this one.

"A trigger, a trigger." Arty flexed and un-flexed his index finger.

"THAT'S g-good." Bill snickered and shook his head. "A friggin trigger."

"It was all very mysterious and we were so drunk it spooked me at first. Now, I think it's pretty interesting. It means I'll have had a purpose, even if I don't know what it is myself."

"I think it means she took your ten bucks and gave you a nice ride, pal." Kirby lit a cigarette with the butt of his last one.

149

"What did she tell Cordell?" Smitty raised up on one elbow.

"She told him he was lucky," Arty said quietly.

"Didn't say whether it was good luck or bad?" Smitty wiped sweat off his forehead with the back of his hand.

"Well, Cordell assumed it was good luck. Things always fell in place for him. He was the golden boy you know."

"How's that?" Grogan had never met Cordell, Bill realized.

"He always WON everything," Smitty remembered. "Contests, races, lotteries. His footlocker is full of shit he won from playing craps and pinochle and checkers."

"He always got the b-best looking women too." Bill thought about Ioké.

"He always got ALL the women, good looking AND the dogs. They loved him." Arty tried to stretch out one leg but accidentally bumped Grogan who jumped and swung his rifle around.

"And he loved them right back, that hound." Smitty clicked his tongue against his teeth. "Never left any for me. That's why he set me up with his sister, for crying out loud. At least SHE gave me a chance. The others took one look at ole Cordell and I was part of the woodwork."

"Yep, he was always at the right place at the right time." Arty twisted trying to get comfortable. "He BELIEVED in his luck too. Counted on it."

"Right up until it let him down." Kirby sighed.

"Damn, my stomach's all tore up again." Smitty doubled over and clutched his belly.

"Stay d-down and hold it." It scared Bill the way that Smitty was moaning and rolling around.

"I'm down, I'm down already -- but I can't stay down here much longer. They better get that bastard soon."

No longer able to keep his lanky frame folded, Arty raised his head a few inches above the edge of the ridge where they were hidden. The gunner sprayed the area with fire. He ducked down. "Doesn't look like we can do anything from here. He's right in front of us."

Bill covered his head with his arms as if that would ward off a bullet with his name on it. "Where are those g-guys with the flamethrower?"

"I didn't see them, but they've got to be coming sooner or later. There are at least twenty other guys out there, pinned down by this freak."

"They'll call in a tank or a plane to firebomb that cave," Kirby said. "We just have to be patient."

"They'll have to work their way around to the side to get him." Smitty groaned. "That could take forever."

"You stay put." Arty shook a long finger at him.

"I can't hold it much longer, guys." Smitty writhed, trying to control his bowels.

"Then pull your pants down and do it here. Just keep low."

"I'm not crapping in front of you guys."

"It's b-better than d-dying in front of us." Bill didn't like the idea of it any better than Smitty, but there were no reasonable alternatives.

"This place stinks bad enough. And I don't want to lay in it, for crying out loud."

"Then h-hold it. Concentrate."

"Maybe if I scoot backwards he won't see me." Smitty

151

inched backwards, but then suddenly curled up into a tight ball to ride out the cramp.

"Damnit, Smitty. You are a pain in the ass." Bill muttered through clinched teeth.

"I know, Zim. I'm sorry. I can't help it."

Smitty's desperation melted Bill's irritation. "I know you can't. But, d-dammit, what are we going to d-do about you?"

"Maybe Doc has something that'll help," Kirby suggested.

"Doc's got b-better things to do than risk his ass for someone with diarrhea, besides he'd get shot b-before he got near us."

"Let's talk about something else. Maybe that will help me forget about it." Smitty farted wetly in spite of himself.

They were silent for a while. The battle raged in the distance. Here there were just sporadic shots until someone rose up too high out of their hiding places. Then the gunner let go.

"I don't know what to talk about." Kirby's fingers trembled as he lit still another cigarette. "I can't stand to think about what's happening now, but it's worse to think about home."

Thoughts of Bailey Hill made Bill feel wistful. Hanging out with RL on the front porch, chasing chickens around the back yard, playing cards with Grandpa Sam. He blinked back the moisture in his eyes. "You have a g-girlfriend, Kirby?"

"I'm engaged. If she'll still have me." His voice trailed off and the boys grew quiet.

Bill closed his eyes. Why Kirby's fiancé wouldn't still want him, he wondered. Had Kirby changed that much? Yeah, he probably had Bill realized. They all had. He thought about the piece of bone in his pocket, about the ring on Cordell's finger, about the nameless dead Japanese soldier. After all of this, would anything ever be okay again? Would home be the same now? Would any girl ever want him?

Arty broke the silence. "We've been here a long time now -- and we only got about a third of this godforsaken island. We've lost almost half of the guys that came in with us in one way or another and I've yet to see a live Jap up close. I'm getting sick of this stinking place. What IS that smell anyway?"

"Sulfur," Bill said. "L-like in Hell."

"Right. Sulfur."

Grogan rolled over onto his back. "What the hell is THAT?" A big plane lumbered towards the airfield to their right. "That's not a transport."

Kirby twisted his head. "That's a B-29! This island is still hot. Surely they aren't going to land here now." The plane came in on the west side of Suribachi and touched down on the south end of the runway. As it skidded down the runway, Japanese mortars and artillery shells focused on it.

"DAMN, can you b-believe that?"

"Probably coming back from bombing the mainland," Arty guessed.

"Why would they land here of all places?" Grogan inched backwards up the slope to get a better look. "Wouldn't just about anywhere else be safer?"

"Maybe they were running out of gas?"

"GUYS, I GOTTA GO!" Kendall Smith struggled to his feet and tried to run. The gunner caught him full in the chest and he fell back down onto his screaming friends. Liquid feces ran down his legs. Several bullets went right through him.

"OH GOD, SMITTY. NOT YOU." Bill turned him over and

153

tried to close the gaping chest wound with his hands. Smitty struggled to breathe and his eyes glassed over.

"CORPSMAN! CORPSMAN!" Arty cupped his hands around his mouth.

"CORPSMAN!" Kirby took up the call.

"I can't close this damned wound." Bill's hands were shaking. "I can't hold it together."

Arty rummaged in his belly pack. "Sprinkle this on it." He handed Bill a packet of sulfa drugs.

"Shit, shit, shit." Kirby wiped tears out of his eyes with his knuckle while the Japanese continued their attempts to destroy the B-29.

Bill sprinkled the powder over the wound. "I don't know what I'm doing, Arty. What if I'm doing it wrong?"

"Use this. Maybe it will close it." Arty held out a three-inch safety pin.

Bill took it and slipped it through the torn flesh on one side of the massive wound. Pulling it through to the other side, he clipped it together. Foamy blood spewed out of Smitty's nose and mouth. "Hang in there, b-buddy. Don't you die. You hear me. Don't you d-die."

"Can't help it." The harelip scar under Smitty's nose turned white and then bluish.

"SMITTY. Damn you!" Bill shuddered as the pink foam spilled over his hands.

"Where's Doc? Where the hell is Doc?" Arty stuck his head up and looked around. The gun spurted again. He ducked back down. "I can't even see Kline." He pounded the side of the shell hole with his fist in frustration.

"It's t-too late anyway." Bill cradled Smitty in his lap,

crouched low to avoid the machine gunner. "It's too late."

Smitty convulsed, his body bucking and fighting for life. It took thirty-eight minutes for Kendall Smith to die. When it was over, Bill took the Japanese pistol off of Smitty's body and put it in his belt.

An hour later, a Marine dive-bomber flew in very low over their heads and dropped a skip bomb that bounced across the ground into the cave. It exploded with a tremendous roar. The men moved forward.

Chapter 9 -- Kirby

One day bled into the next. The boys labored on, trying to survive. Arty grew sad and morose. Bill grew angrier. Kirby just got quiet. Replacements came and died. They pushed further up the western side of the island.

"When is this going to stop?" Bill wondered the night after Grogan was killed near hill 362 A

"I don't know, buddy." Arty's slouch had grown more pronounced.

"I don't think I c-can stand it anymore. I'm afraid to sleep or pee or even b-blink." Bill bit his lower lip.

"It's the stench that gets to me. It does smell like hell. Sulfur and rotting bodies." Arty fingered the silver mezuzah he wore around his neck. His thickening beard was crusted with lint and sand.

Bill and Kirby and Arty crouched in a foxhole. They were so close to the enemy they could hear the ping when each mortar fired. Ever so often, they heard the wounded screaming for a corpsman.

"I think d-dead Japs smell worse than dead M-Marines."

"They are probably saying the opposite, Zim." Kirby had grown thinner and his red beard had streaks of silver in it.

"I could h-hear them last night. Underneath us."

"Those tunnels must be cozy away from the cold and the

shelling. Pop up, kill a few Marines. Move on. They say that's why we keep getting slammed from behind. We take a pillbox and go past it. Then the Japs use the tunnels and crawl back in to shoot us," Arty said.

"That would be a damned lousy place to die though -- underground. Where d-do these sonuvabitches c-come from?" Bill waved his hands at a swarm of black flies.

"You got blood and dead bodies, you got flies," Arty said and shrugged.

"I don't even care if I get shot any more." Kirby folded his arms over his chest to keep warm. "If you don't get it today, you'll get it tomorrow. What are our chances of ever leaving this island alive, really?"

"Maybe the best we can do is die well," Arty said. "They say the Japs think they achieve salvation by dying well."

"How do you d-die well?" Arty had some of the strangest ideas. Dying was dying to Bill -- bloody and ugly.

"If you die bravely or for your country or some such shit."

"Then I guess C-Cordell and Kroner and Smitty and G-Grogan and -- what was that kid's name? Stewart? I guess they all achieved salvation then." Bill was sarcastic.

"Maybe it was just their time, Zim. Maybe there is a plan or something."

"Cordell was just lucky?"

"Something like that."

"Maybe God was calling him home," Kirby said softly.

"At least he didn't have to w-watch his friends die one by one." Bill folded his arms over his chest. "Seems to me that is one m-mean b-bastard running this show."

"I dunno. We must be alive for some reason, Zim. How many close calls have we had? Getting past D-Day was a major achievement. Maybe we are meant to survive this thing." Arty touched his mezuzah.

"How can you accept all this as fate?" Bill waved his hand over the battlefield. "Seems like an incredible w-waste to m-me."

"Me too." Kirby took off his legging and shoe to rub his swollen ankle. He had hurt it several days earlier. "I keep trying to hold on to what I used to believe. To who I was. I think about my mom. Does she know I'm here? I've got two brothers in the Marines and an uncle fighting in Europe. I don't even know where they are now."

"Well at first I figured I'd die on this stinking island but here we are after all this time. So for some reason, I'm hopeful for the first time since D-Day. I think we're gonna make it. Maybe my mother will have grandchildren after all." Arty's optimism in the face of such slaughter confused and annoyed Bill.

"I forgot how to hope," Kirby murmured.

A shell exploded nearby lighting up the night sky with a blistering ball of fire. Another blast and the boys heard more cries for help outside their foxhole. Still another explosion, closer. Hot rocks and coarse sand hit Kirby in the face, cutting and burning his right eye. He wiped debris from his face with the dirty sleeve of his shirt.

"Kirby?" Arty touched his shoulder.

"I'm fine, fellas." Kirby had been different since he got cut off from the rest of them for a couple of days. He'd always been quiet, but now there was desperation in his silence that frightened Bill -- frightened him because he recognized it.

The artillery and mortar fire continued but slowed as the sun rose over the battlefield. Someone dropped K-rations into the hole for them. The boys cut into the boxes to retrieve cigarettes, but ignored the food.

Bill watched Kirby light up with trembling hands. "You b-better get that shoe back on, buddy."

"Oh, yeah. Sure." Kirby struggled to get the boot back on his swollen foot.

"Here." Arty took the boot from Kirby, pulled the shoestring out and handed it back. Kirby slipped it on, wincing as the leather touched his foot. Arty cut a small piece of the shoestring and used it at the very top of Kirby's boot.

"OKAY, boys. Let's get moving." Another new sergeant stuck his head over the foxhole.

"Sarge, do you have any APC tablets? My ankle is killing me." Kirby crawled out of the foxhole, shading his eyes against the morning sun with his arm. Arty and Bill followed.

"You look like shit, Private. What the hell were you doing? Fist fighting? Your eye looks like a fucking tomato. And what's wrong with your ankle?" They had just met the sergeant the night before. None of them knew his first name.

"I don't know. I must have twisted it or something." Kirby seemed dazed.

Another shell exploded knocking them down and partly covering them with rocks and sand. Bill sat up and brushed the dirt off of his legs. Arty was chasing something round. What was it? Kirby's helmet?

Bill turned to his right. Kirby lay spread-eagled, his red hair fluttering in the breeze. "Oh My God, Kirby! Kirby! Look at him." Bill snapped his fingers in front of Kirby's face.

"CORPSMAN!" The sergeant screamed.

Bill and Arty stood guard over Kirby until Doc Kline came.

"What the hell is going on now?" Kneeling, Doc pulled each of Kirby's eyes open with a thumb on the lower lid. He leaned back on his heels and sighed. "We gotta get him out of here."

"Is he dead?"

"He's banged up, but we can fix that. He's in shock -- doesn't even know who he is."

The sergeant nodded. "I'll call in someone to get him out on a litter."

"What's going to h-happen to him, Doc?" Bill laid Kirby's cigarettes on his chest. "Is he going to be okay?"

"Who knows?" Doc Kline took off his helmet and wiped his forehead.

Bill blinked. Doc was losing his hair. He wasn't even out of his teens yet and he was going bald. It didn't seem right.

"Let's get out of here, men. There's a war going on." The sergeant gave Bill a little push.

Bill scowled at him. Did the sonuvabitch think they didn't know where they were or what was happening? The young man's cheeks flushed and Bill felt bad for him. Maybe the Sarge was so damn green he didn't know what to say.

Bill sighed and nodded.

Leaning over, he tapped Kirby on the head.

No response.

The boys shouldered their packs and rifles and trudged off behind the new sergeant leaving Kirby behind with Doc Kline. Bill turned to look back only once.

Chapter 10 -- The Last Day

On March 19, the boys found themselves in front of a knoll. The enemy guns fell silent. Demolitions men blasted one cave entrance closed. Machine gunners killed Japanese soldiers who ran from a back entrance. Marines swarmed up over the hill in triumph and curiosity.

"Looks like we got this thing licked," Arty said. "Let's go up there with those guys."

"It scares me, Arty. Something's not r-right."

"Scares you?"

"I c-can't explain it. The d-damned hill scares me."

"Then I won't go up there. I'll stay with you."

"G-Good."

There was a tremendous blast. The top of the hill in front of them blew off. Bill and Arty were knocked off their feet by the concussion. Dozens of Marines disappeared into the crater. The Japanese had blown up one of their command posts in a cavern under the hill.

Bill and Arty ran up the slope and starting digging into the steaming earth, trying to find Marines who had fallen into the crater. The bodies were burned black and smoking.

"Goddamned Japs!" Bill pulled a young boy out of the smoldering heap of dirt. The scorched flesh came away from the bone when Bill tried to lift the body.

"How did you know, Zim?"

"I d-don't know. I just felt scared."

They tugged on the blackened leg of a corpse.

"This could have been me, pal." Arty shivered as they pulled the body clear of the rocks. "Maybe the fix is in with the big Guy."

"Don't say that. Don't t-tempt fate." Now Bill felt superstitious.

"If a bullet has my name on it, I'm done anyway."

"Well, let's just c-concentrate on staying alive."

"I'm sticking with you, brother." Arty laid a hand on Bill's shoulder. "You got the nose for trouble now. I'm putting my hopes on you."

●●●●●

The boys trekked down a rocky pathway between two cliffs. It was so tight they had to walk single file. They were with three replacements. The new Marines seemed very young and clean. Cliff Barton had rejoined them as well.

"So you guys came in on D-Day?" Scooter Day asked as they picked their way through the rocky gully.

"Yeah." Bill tried not to talk to the new ones. It didn't pay to get attached because they died off so quickly.

"I'm tired. Can't you guys slow down?" Barton whined.

"Was it as bad as they say?" Scooter asked.

"Yeah." Bill led the group. Barton was behind him, the three new boys followed and Arty brought up the rear.

They found an empty cave and threw grenades into it just to be sure. They inspected the hollow carved into the rock. A pile of rubble towards the back told them where the exit had been. It was empty. Nothing left but a bunch of dead bats.

They backed out and headed for the next area.

Bill glanced back over his shoulder. "Where's Arty?"

"He's right behind me." A round-faced boy from Virginia turned around to look for Arty.

Arty wasn't there.

"ARTY?" Bill called. "ARTY! Where are you, pal?"

There was no answer.

"NOOOOOO." Bill dashed past the new boys who stood frozen on the path and headed for the cave.

"Well, if we are going to play hide and seek, I'm going to take a load off." Barton sat down and opened his pack. "Think I'll have a little snack." The three boys watched Barton bite into a chocolate bar. Then they sat down with him.

Bill approached the cave. There was movement at the mouth -- and screaming -- horrible, endless screaming in Arty's voice. Two men in Japanese uniforms bent over something on the ground. They were the first live Japanese soldiers Bill had seen up close. He squatted and fired several shots in their direction. They disappeared into the back of the cave.

He scuttled across the landscape, his butt near the ground, his head down and peered into the cave. It was empty. The Japanese had disappeared back into one of their hidden tunnels.

Arty lay on his back clutching his broken glasses with one hand and his mid-section with the other. His howls become voiceless, his eyes dull. The wound ran from his sternum down to his pubic bone. His intestines had been pulled out of his body cavity and were curled in the dirt beside him. Deep gashes ran up each thigh and they had cut off his nose.

"Arty!" Bill could hardly get the word out.

"Zim, they got me good." Blood poured out of Arty's body in all directions and his left foot jerked spasmodically.

"I'll go get Doc Kline."

"No, No, No! Don't leave me, Zim!" Arty's voice rose to just above a whisper. "Remember, you said you'd stay with me? There's not time anyway." He gritted his teeth.

"I ain't going no where, buddy." Bill knelt beside Arty and held his hand.

"You won't tell my mom about this will you?" Arty's body quivered.

"I ain't telling her shit."

"You gotta help me. I think they cut my dick off. I need you to see if they cut it off. I can't seem to make myself look."

"Naw, buddy. You are fine." Bill was calm. Arty's penis lay a few feet from his body where the soldiers had dropped it when Bill chased them away.

"Good, then there's still hope my mother will have grandchildren." Tears ran down Arty's nose-less face.

"Yeah, pal. There's hope." Bill pressed the Japanese pistol against Arty's temple and fired.

A Grateful Nation

Traffic was bumper to bumper on Water Street. Sunlight reflected off the hood of the El Camino and into Bill's eyes. He squinted and tapped the accelerator. The truck inched forward. Damned kid. He'd talked until he was blue in the face, but it was like conversing with a rock. College was no place for a girl -- especially HIS daughter, especially now with all this craziness going on.

"Are you a sympathizer?" A chubby woman standing on the sidewalk yelled at him through his passenger window.

"A w-what?"

"Coming in from out of state to get even?"

Bill scowled. "Do I look like a k-kid?"

"They say the communists are going to disguise themselves as guardsmen."

"I'm not a communist OR a g-guardsman. Used to be a Marine though."

She wrinkled her nose. "You don't look like a Marine to me."

The Pontiac in front of him moved. Bill threw the gearshift into low. The wheels on the El Camino squealed and the truck lurched forward. The car in front stopped after five feet. Bill stood on his brakes, cursing.

"We're decent God-fearing people in this town," The

woman screamed after him. "We don't want outside agitators causing more trouble. You aren't welcome here, do you hear me?"

Bill stared through the windshield, fighting the urge to show her his middle finger through the back window.

"YOU HEAR ME?"

Damn stupid Yankees. His out of state license branded him in this fucked up town. Why the hell did Hope run off up here of all places? Traffic moved again and he turned onto Main. This was no better. At the next corner, a red-eared young cop leaned in the window. "Name?"

"Bill Zimmer."

"State your business." The name tag on the cop's chest said *Hernandez*.

"Trying to get in to pick up my d-daughter and take her home."

"Is she expecting you?"

Officer Hernandez smelled like that expensive aftershave the kids were using these days. It made Bill's sinuses throb. "Well, since the phone system is screwed up I d-doubt it."

The policeman tapped the roof of the El Camino with his billie club. "Move on."

"How am I supposed to find my d-daughter?"

"MOVE ON!"

DAMMIT! Bill had been circling Kent State University for nearly two hours trying to get to Hope's dorm. The fact that he hadn't heard from her since the shooting made his stomach roll during the long drive up from Fort Smith. He wouldn't let himself think about what he might do if she wasn't in her room.

As if to emphasize the infinite power of the United States Government in general and the state of Ohio in particular, dozens of unsmiling troops stood their posts while scared parents hustled their long-haired kids past them. A soldier standing on a city sidewalk holding a rifle followed Bill with his eyes. Bill pretended not to notice but sweat trickled down between his shoulder blades. Kent wasn't Fort Smith and he didn't like being away from home even in the best of times.

He didn't blame the guardsmen for shooting the little bastards. You couldn't have kids tearing up personal property, sassing their betters, refusing to go when drafted. Where would the country be if kids wouldn't fight? He hadn't wanted to fight the Japs at first either, but he never considered disobeying. Every one pulled together back then.

Up ahead, a shiny blue and white Volkswagen bus pulled out into traffic, leaving a parking space. It was a tight fit, but Bill wasn't going to go around the block one more time. Ignoring the loud chorus of bleating horns behind him, Bill squeezed the El Camino into the tiny slot even though it took two tries.

"IDIOT!" The driver behind shouted as he drove past.

"You w-want some of this?" Bill shook his fist.

The other man slammed on his brakes and jumped out of his car. "Come on, asshole."

Bill threw open the door of the El Camino, grabbed a tire iron from behind his seat and charged. "I'll smash your fucking face in." The metal bar swished through the air inches from his tormentor's nose.

"THAT'S ENOUGH!" The soldier on the sidewalk leveled a rifle at them.

Bill dropped the tire iron.

167

The other driver backed off, his hands in the air. "Don't shoot. I got a family to take care of."

Unmoved, the soldier stared at them over the quivering barrel of his rifle. In a flash, two cops from opposite ends of the block converged on the scene. "Get moving, Oscar." Officer Hernandez pushed the bigger man back toward his car. "Go on now, your wife will be pissed off if you go home with your head split open."

As Officer Hernandez steered Oscar back to his car, the other cop positioned himself between Bill and the soldier's rifle. "Get back in your car, sir," he said.

"I want to go g-get my daughter."

"Look, everyone's on edge around here." This man was older than Officer Hernandez, older than Bill even -- a sergeant. "Look at that boy over there with a gun," he said. "He's scared to death."

Bill glanced at the soldier. "I'm not afraid of him."

"You ought to be."

"I was a M-Marine."

"Then you should know how dangerous a scared kid with a loaded gun can be."

Bill lowered his eyes. "My d-daughter lives in Prentice Hall. Her mother is about c-crazy over all of this."

"Look," the sergeant said. "We want you to get her out of here but starting fights in the middle of the street isn't going to help you do that. Folks are upset and edgy. There's already been one tragedy."

"So how d-do I get in there?"

"What's her name?"

"Hope Zimmer. She's a little g-girl. About like this." Bill held his hand at eyebrow level.

The cop pressed a key on his walkie-talkie. "Arnold?"

"Yeah." The radio crackled.

"How far are you from Prentice Hall?"

"Fifty yards."

"Go see if there's a Hope Zimmer listed."

"Okay."

Bill's sinuses ached. He patted his breast pocket looking for the little red and white squeeze bottle. Not there. He squinted at the cop's name tag. "Can I get my m-medicine out of the car, Sergeant Cooper?"

"You aren't going to pull any funny stuff on me, are you?"

"Look, I'm not the b-bad guy here. I just want to find my k-kid."

The cop nodded. Bill opened the car door and felt around on the seat. There it was. The pressure over his eyebrows was almost too intense to bear. He grabbed the little bottle of Dristan and holding one nostril closed with an index finger, he squirted the medication up the other. He sniffed. "AHHH."

Sergeant Cooper stood with his arms folded over his chest watching Bill. "Better?"

"I have this p-problem with headaches," Bill said.

The radio came alive. "Sarge?"

"Yeah?"

"Hope Zimmer was shot. She's at Robinson."

Blood drained from Bill's face and he felt lightheaded. Someone shot his baby? Images of gruesome gunshot wounds flickered through his mind and he fell backwards against the El Camino.

"Thanks," Sergeant Cooper keyed the mic and hooked the radio back on his belt. Turning to Bill, he said, "Are you okay?"

"What's Robinson?" Bill held his breath, praying it wasn't a funeral home.

"Robinson Memorial. It's the closest hospital. Leave your car here and I'll get you there in a cruiser." The cop's big hand closed around Bill's bicep but his eyes were kind and his voice softer now.

"No, I'll d-drive myself."

"You're a mess, Mr. Zimmer. I can't let you drive right now. Your car will be okay parked here."

Bill nodded and let Sergeant Cooper guide him down the street to a black and white Chevy.

● ● ● ● ●

Bill stood outside the door of Hope's room on the surgical ward. She wasn't in danger, the nurse had told him but she was going to need surgery to rebuild her foot. He was relieved but still upset. What kind of idiot would shoot a little girl like Hope? Still, the National Guard represented the government. They couldn't have made a mistake. The government never made mistakes. She must have been doing something wrong. She'd always been a rebellious kid. She probably sassed the Guardsmen when they told her to leave. He wouldn't put it past her -- but did they have to shoot her?

He laid his forehead on the door. What would he say to her? How worried he'd been for her safety? How glad he was that she was okay? How furious he was that someone shot her? How embarrassing he found her politics? How hurt he was that she left home? He took the Dristan out of his pocket and medicated himself again. Okay. He was ready. He pushed open the door and went in.

Hope lay on the bed with her thin arms on top of the covers. A young man with very long hair was leaning over her, his bearded face close to hers. She'd turned her head away from him as though she were trying to avoid his lips.

The bastard was trying to KISS her! Bill grabbed the back of the boy's shirt and pulled him away from the bed. "Who the h-hell are you?"

The young man's eyes widened. "Who are you?" The alarm in his face was satisfying. After all he'd been through since he heard of the shootings Bill wanted to punish someone. This long haired subversive made a great target. Bill clenched his fists.

"Daddy!" Hope struggled to sit up.

"Mr. Zimmer?" The boy backed away.

"What are you doing to my d-daughter?"

"Barry's my friend, Daddy. He's here to take care of me."

Bill glanced at Hope. Her face was pale and there was a large bruise on her forehead. "D-doesn't look like he's done a very g-good job." He clenched his fists. "What k-kind of name is Berry? Sounds like a fruit to me."

"Not Berry," Hope rasped as if she had a cold. "BARRY!"

Barry held up both hands, showing Bill his palms. "Please Mr. Zimmer. Hope's had a bad time of it. Let's not make it worse by fighting."

"Was it you who g-got her in trouble? Led her out there where they were shooting?"

"Barry was in Cleveland yesterday. He wasn't even here." Hope reached out to touch Bill's arm. "He came back as soon as

171

he heard I was hurt and stayed here with me all night."

Bill wasn't sure he liked the idea of this hairball spending any time at all with Hope. "You c-could have c-called us."

Barry tried last night for hours." She winced and relaxed back into the sheets. "The phones were messed up."

At least the kid did that. Now that Bill thought about it, Hope must have been scared. It was nice of this Barry fellow to see to it that she wasn't alone in this strange place. Maybe he wasn't so bad after all. Bill stuck out his hand. "I'm sorry," he said. "For b-before."

"It's okay, sir. I'd be upset too, under the circumstances." Barry's handshake was surprisingly firm but Bill still didn't like his looks.

Turning his back on Barry, Bill said to Hope, "How do you feel?"

"I hurt."

"Can't they g-give you something?"

"It makes me fall asleep. They have a surgeon coming in from Cleveland. I want to stay awake until he gets here."

"I think that I'll go now that your dad is here." Barry patted Hope's hand.

"Okay," Hope said. "Thanks for everything."

"I'll be back later."

"You don't have to."

"I want to," he said and closed the door behind him.

Hope sighed. "Fine."

Bill was glad the hairy bastard was gone. He wanted Hope all to himself. "They told me that you will n-need surgery."

"Yes."

The silence between them wasn't new but it was still loud.

"Are you going to t-tell me what happened?"

She closed her eyes. "They came on campus and shot us."

"Don't sass m-me."

"Those are the facts. What do you want? Truth?"

For the life of him, he never understood the difference and her insistence that there WAS one made him feel stupid. "The t-truth would be n-nice."

"I was on my way home from class."

He frowned. "They said on TV that the p-protesters were throwing r-rocks."

"I don't know. I didn't see them."

"You weren't p-protesting?"

"Not yesterday. Not when I was shot."

He felt his neck and ears getting hot. It wasn't right. His own daughter involved in such things. He'd never thought something like this would have happened, of course, but he knew going off to college so far away from home was a bad idea. "Why d-do you have to d-do this to me?"

She turned her head on the pillow and stared out the window. "You sound like Barry."

He gritted his teeth. "How d-do I sound l-like that hippy?"

She laughed but it sounded like crying. "Hippy? Oh, that's a good one."

"For G-God's sake, Hope!" He gripped her bed railing and shook it. "SAY what you m-mean. Enough of this beating around the b-bush b-bullshit."

"Barry is a Marine," she said. "Like you."

"W-what?" He couldn't believe it.

"Just back from Nam a few months ago." She snorted. "It's ironic. The two of you have so much in common."

He sat down in a straight backed chair beside her bed. It was all so confusing. He never knew who was who anymore. "A b-boyfriend?"

"No."

"B-bullshit. He's in love with you."

"So he says."

"But n-not you?"

"I care but I'm not going to live with a man who's been in combat and I don't want him to hope for more. It wouldn't be fair."

He took the blow without flinching but it was like a knife in the heart. "What's w-wrong with a veteran?"

"Nothing. It's just not what I want." She still refused to look at him.

He thought about what it was like in 1944. Women loved men in uniform then. "Maybe I misjudged B-berry. A young man coming back from w-war deserves to be wanted -- to have someone w-waiting for him at home."

"His name is Barry, Daddy."

"Fine. Barry."

"You drove all night?"

"I left as soon as I heard about this deal. Your m-mother was w-worried."

She turned her head and caught his eye. "Mama was

worried?"

"I was w-worried."

She stretched out her hand and he took it. "Thanks, Daddy."

"I would rather l-lock you up in your room for the rest of your life than have had this h-happen to you."

The corners of her mouth twitched. "You can't keep bad things from happening to me."

He squeezed her hand. "I tried."

"I know you did." Her dark eyes filled with tears.

"Will you c-come home now?"

"Maybe for a little while until my foot heals. Then I have to go back to school. "

Her obstinacy, even now after all that had happened, overwhelmed him. "What did I d-do that was so wrong?"

A quick rap on the door and then it opened. A white-coated man limped into the room, his rubber soles squeaking on the tile. "Hello, Miss Zimmer. I'm Doctor Kline. They called me down to take a look at you and see what can be done about that foot."

"Hello, Doctor. This is my father. We've been waiting for you."

"Dan Kline, Mr. Zimmer."

Bill dropped Hope's hand and stood up. "Danny? Danny Kline?"

The surgeon peered at Bill over his half-glasses. "Zim?"

"It's me, Doc."

"My God, Zim. I can't believe it." Doc Kline pulled Bill into an awkward hug.

"I never heard what happened to you, Doc. I was afraid you'd -- I'm g-glad to see that you are okay." Aware of Hope's shocked eyes on them, Bill endured the embarrassing embrace relieved to know that Danny Kline at least was alive.

"I'm fine." Doc released Bill and stepped back. "They got me off the island and onto a hospital ship within hours. I'll never sprint again, of course." He slapped his own thigh and laughed. "But I get around fine."

"I'm glad." Bill blew air through his lips remembering the day a grenade landed a few feet from where Doc was tending a wounded man. Shrapnel from the explosion killed the injured Marine and shredded Doc's leg.

"Thanks to you."

Bill blushed. "I wish I could have done m-more."

"You saved my life, Zim." For a moment, this bald headed stranger sounded like the old Danny Kline. "There's not a day goes by that I'm not grateful that it was you who found me."

Not wanting to get into this kind of conversation in front of Hope, Bill changed the subject. "So you are a real doctor now?"

"GI Bill."

"That's wonderful. You are the b-best." As a Navy Corpsman, Danny Kline risked his life every day for weeks on Iwo Jima to help other people. It seemed right that he should get to be a doctor. At least something was right in this crazy world, Bill thought.

"It's a good life now," Doc said.

They smiled at each other but neither seemed to know what to say next. There were no safe topics in their past -- and Hope was their only connection now.

"How b-bad is Hope's foot?"

Doc turned back to Hope. "I've been studying the file and X-rays. Let's take a look at what we have and I'll let you know."

Bill swallowed. "I'll step outside during the exam, if you don't mind."

"It's okay, Daddy. I'll be fine," Hope said but Bill recognized that pinched little look she got when she was scared and his heart twisted in his chest. He inched backwards but couldn't make himself leave the room. He'd let her down when he let her leave Fort Smith, like he let everyone else down -- his mother, Little Mack, RL, Smitty -- Arty. He wasn't going to let Hope face this alone no matter what it cost him to stay here and watch.

"Let me get a nurse to help out," Doc said as he pressed the call button. "It's time to put on a fresh dressing anyway."

Hope sucked air through her teeth and paled as Doc pulled back the covers and began unwrapping the bandages on her left foot.

Bill pressed himself against the wall near her bed. She glanced up at him. "Doctor Kline will take care of me. I know you don't like stuff like this."

He took her hand. "No, I want to be here."

She exhaled and her fingers tightened around his.

• • • • •

He sat down near the window in the waiting room, sprayed Dristan up his nose and lit a Camel. He checked his watch. Hope had been in surgery for four hours now. How much longer could it be? He tried not to think about what that bullet did to her foot. She'd been so pink and perfect when she was born. He remembered touching each of her toes even though he could see that they were all there. How would he tell her mother that that perfection was gone? Blown away in a

177

moment of idiocy?

"Do you mind?"

Bill preferred solitude but he shook his head.

Barry sat down across from him. "I know we got off on the wrong foot, Mr. Zimmer."

Bill shrugged.

"I want you to know that I'd have died rather than have this happen to Hope." The boy had showered and changed clothes, but there were dark circles under his eyes and he looked exhausted.

"Who ARE you, B-berry?"

"A failure."

Bill snickered. "Welcome to the c-club."

"That's why she won't have me."

"That's n-not what she said."

A loud crash. They both flinched. A hospital worker knelt to pick up the tray of food she'd dropped. They looked at each other and relaxed.

Bill flicked an ash into a glass dish. "Where were you?"

"Khe Sanh. You?"

"Iwo."

"Damn."

Bill fished the pack of Camels out of his chest pocket. "Want a cigarette?"

"Thanks."

They were on their third cigarette when Doc Kline appeared at the door.

"How is she, Doc?" Barry stood up.

"She's in recovery now. There was significant damage, as you know, but I was able to save the foot, I think -- barring post operative infection."

Bill covered his eyes with his hand trying not to cry with relief.

"She did as well as we could expect," Doc continued, "and I think we accomplished what we set out to do. Time will tell if she gets back all the feeling. We'll let her heal awhile and then tackle the task of getting her walking again."

"Can I see her?" Barry looked from Bill to Doc and back to Bill.

"She's not quite awake yet," Doc said.

"That's okay. I just want to be there when she opens her eyes." Barry fidgeted from one foot to the other.

Bill took a drag off his cigarette and nodded.

"She's down the hall, third door on the left, Doc said. "Tell Lucy that I said you could stay with her."

"Thanks, Doc. Thanks, Mr. Zimmer."

"Nice young man," Doc said when Barry was gone.

"I g-guess."

"Were we ever that young?" He sat down in Barry's chair.

"Not for l-long."

"Remember how beautiful everything was in Hawaii? We played in the surf like children." Doc leaned back in the chair and stretched.

"I h-hated the water."

"That's right. I remember now. Why was that?"

"I dunno. I don't like being in over my h-head, I guess."

Doc chuckled. "We sure had some good times though. Remember Jimmy's? Smitty made that beat-up piano sound like a baby grand. Cordell would be dancing cheek to cheek with some little cutie while Lieberman sat at the bar and went on and on about politics or religion or whatever. They were a good bunch of boys."

Bill nodded. They were indeed. Too bad they were mostly dead. "Whatever h-happened to that snake, Cliff Barton?"

"He's the mayor of a small town in Texas, would you believe?" Doc laughed.

"He's probably stealing them b-blind."

"From what I hear he's going to run for congress next year."

"Figures," Bill grunted thinking about how unfair it was that good guys like his friends died back on that stinking island and he and Barton walked away without a scratch.

"I saw Lieberman's family back in the early 1950s," Doc said as if reading his mind. "Nice folks. His mother was still blaming herself for his death."

"W-why w-would she d-do that?"

"Well, seems like Lieberman was going to join the army. He wanted to get Hitler personally. But his mother was afraid that if he got captured by the Germans, it would go bad for him being Jewish and all."

"So he became a M-marine."

"Imagine that."

"Damn."

Doc got up. "Well, I need to get back to Cleveland for now. I'll be back tomorrow to check on Hope, but I think she will be fine."

"Thank you, Doc. I'm l-lucky you were here."

"It's the least I could do for you, Zim." Doc limped toward the door.

Bill followed after him. "You know, when we first c-came home I r-really felt g-good about what we d-did over there. I h-hung onto that when things g-got bad."

"But it's different now?"

"N-no one knows w-what w-we did -- n-not really. And they aren't even all that g-grateful anymore. I mean when I g-got into town some woman c-called me an outside agitator. I c-couldn't believe it."

Doc shook his head. "She had no idea who she was talking to."

"It still h-hurt. After all we went through I w-would have thought no one w-would question my r-right to b-be anywhere in this country. And then -- all these k-kids protesting makes me m-mad."

"Why?"

"That's just it. I d-don't know why."

Doc pressed the elevator button. "Seems to me they are just exercising the rights that we fought for, Zim -- despite how things turned out here at Kent."

"I know, but it m-makes me feel b-bad again. L-like I did something wrong. I d-don't want to think that the g-government could make m-mistakes. I d-don't want to question what we did over there. I d-don't want to think that our friends died for n-no reason."

181

"I'm not sure anyone who wasn't there can ever know what happened. I'm not sure I want them to know."

Bill studied his fingernails. "Me either."

"And we can't know what's happening in Nam now. One thing's for sure, I don't want to waste any more young lives. Let's pray that the powers that be are right about this war."

"W-what if they aren't, Doc?"

"Only history will tell."

They shook hands and Doc stepped into the elevator.

•••••

"Hi, Daddy." She was propped up in bed with her leg in traction.

"Isn't that uncomfortable?" He pointed to the contraption that held her heavily bandaged foot in the air.

"Not as bad as yesterday when I first woke up after the surgery."

He sat down beside her bed. "B-Barry sent those?"

She glanced at the large bouquet of red roses setting on the dresser across the room and smiled. "Yeah."

"Changing your m-mind about him?"

"Are you?"

"He's a g-good kid, Hope."

"I don't want to be a housewife."

He frowned. "It was g-good enough for your mother."

"It's not what I want. I have other plans."

"That's n-not the real reason, is it?"

She bit her lip as if she were deciding how much to say. "It's one of the real reasons."

He lowered his eyes, unsure if he wanted to push her any further -- yet, he had to know. Other people's kids didn't run off like this. Other girls wanted to get married. "Is it something that I d-did?"

"I don't want to live like you have. "

Her words were soft but they pierced his soul and the pain fed his fury. "I didn't raise you to speak to m-me this way. I didn't raise you to march around a college campus bad-mouthing the government."

"I may not be what you wanted," she retorted, "but I'm exactly what you raised me to be."

It took the wind out of his sails. "I d-did my b-best."

"I know you did. You worked hard and did everything you could for us."

"What is it then?" Bill had spent a lifetime trying and failing. Now he'd lost Hope too. It was too much to bear.

"I love you, Daddy -- and I admire you more than you'll ever know, but I don't want to live with a guy who jumps every time a car backfires, or carries a bone splinter in his wallet, or freaks out when I use a big safety pin for a key chain."

He lowered his eyes, trying to figure out how to explain those things. "It sounds c-crazy the way you p-put it."

"You're not crazy. It's like a wound that never heals, that's all."

"We d-did it for you."

"You didn't do it for me. I wasn't even born yet."

He searched for the reasons. At the time, he didn't know

why the Japanese attacked them or why they were fighting the Germans again. He just knew it was happening and that he had to go fight. "For the c-country -- for freedom," he said but he knew it was more complicated than that.

"Seems to me that freedom is a matter of definition -- some people will always be free, others will always be enslaved. It's inside their heads. For example, you don't seem especially free to me, Daddy -- nor does Barry."

His head throbbed. She made no sense -- she never did. He fingered the Dristan in his pocket. "You c-can't know what happened."

"I've seen what it did to you. The price is high -- too high."

"Other people are g-grateful, p-proud of what we did."

She reached out to him. "I will always be grateful to you, but not for going to war. Time will judge those things -- not me."

He took her hand. "Then w-why?"

"Because you survived."

He recoiled. "That's a horrible thing to say when so many others d-died."

"I exist because you lived, Daddy," she said. "I owe you MY life."

Bill rubbed his aching forehead. "I did some p-pretty awful things to survive."

"Whatever you did, it was worth it."

"There are b-bigger things to consider."

"Not to me."

"And Barry?"

She wiped the corner of her eye with her knuckle. "He beat the odds twice. His father was at Normandy on D-Day and then Barry went to Nam."

"So you've changed your mind about a future with Barry?"

She sniffed and shook her head.

Bill leaned over to kiss her forehead, thinking about all the other children that were never born because of war. Maybe she was right. Maybe in the end, it was about staying alive.

The Brafferton

Gettysburg, Pennsylvania – 2004

Get interested in someone else's war, the doctor had advised. It'll put things in perspective. It'll get you talking. The doctor had it all wrong. Living history wasn't going to help. Kirby parked in the city lot on Stratton Street across from St. James Church and headed back to The Brafferton. He'd enjoyed wandering around the reenactment site with his wife. He hadn't even minded standing outside the Sutler's tents while she bought feathered bonnets and wide petticoats. All the muskets and sabers hadn't bothered him either -- but it was a different story when the cannonade began. Choking back panic, he'd pleaded a headache and left Peg to watch Pickett's Charge with friends.

The traffic light changed as he approached York Street. A young woman in a yellow Honda stopped. Kirby nodded to her before stepping off the curb. He was halfway across the intersection when he heard an engine revving. He whirled as a large truck crashed into the rear of the little car sending it straight toward him.

He locked eyes with the driver. Her mouth was open. When he couldn't stand it anymore, he jumped to the right. The Honda crashed into a pole a few feet away. The woman's head smashed through the windshield and then the truck crushed her little car. Yellow splashed with red and gray was the last thing he saw.

●●●●●

The air conditioner was running full blast. Kirby rolled over onto his back, smacking his lips. Something was caked in the corner of his mouth. Where was he? He sat up and looked around. The Minié ball in the mantle, the slipper bench at the foot of the big cherry bedstead, the armoire -- somehow he was back in his room at The Brafferton.

Throwing back the comforter, he staggered into the bathroom to stare at his reflection in the mirror over the sink. Nothing was broken -- just a cut inside his swollen lower lip. He took a shuddering breath. It made no sense. He was nearing eighty years old yet he was unharmed and the young woman was -- he closed his eyes trying to force his mind to go blank.

It didn't work any more. He bent over the sink and splashed cool water on his face. The images flickered behind his eyes like an old time movie -- big ships bombarding the tiny island, climbing into the rocking Higgins boat, dead bodies scattered on the black beach. A yellow scarf fluttering -- NO!

Dabbing a wet washcloth at the dried blood in the corner of his mouth, Kirby froze as he reentered the bedroom. A stranger in a gray uniform stood by the window peering over the air conditioner down into the street.

"Who the hell are you?"

The figure didn't move. "They can't get her out," he said.

The man seemed at home. Most everyone in Gettysburg dressed in costume during reenactments. Maybe he worked at the inn and had come to the front room on the second floor to watch the excitement -- just another ghoul.

Kirby picked up his wife's roller bag and laid it on the bed. "They can take their time. She's not going to make it."

"Damnation." The man shuddered but kept his eyes on the spectacle in the street. "You ever notice when something

187

happens like that -- something gruesome -- that it's hard to look away even though you want to?"

Kirby had spent a lifetime trying not to look. "How did I get up here?"

"The innkeeper. You were upset. Don't you remember?"

"Vaguely."

A loud crash outside and they both flinched.

"Jaws of life."

The soldier seemed confused. "What?"

"They are tearing the car apart to get to her." Kirby unzipped the side pocket of the bag and stuck his hand inside. Where the hell did Peg pack that baggie?

The sound of screeching metal rose from the street. They eyed each other nervously. Kirby dumped the contents of Peg's bag onto the bed. The soldier watched Kirby sort through the objects on the comforter. "I always did like this room," he said. "Of course, it was a bit different when first I visited."

There it was! Kirby pocketed Peg's bottle of pills. "When was that?"

"Evening of the first day. We got here around three o'clock and pushed the Federals back through town -- killing some, capturing others. I slipped away and wandered through the butcher shop next door. Others had been there before me but I found a scrap of ham they missed and put it in my pocket."

Another actor. Kirby groaned. "Save it until my wife comes back from the reenactment. I'm not in the mood for a performance."

"The family that lived here was gone -- hiding somewhere I guess. They left the front door open. I climbed the stairs. Children's things -- toys, clothes, books -- filled this room. The bed was rumpled as if someone had been napping only a few minutes before. When I bent over to touch the coverlet, some Yankee shot at me. Came through that window right there. Zipped over my head and hit the mantle. If I'd been standing it would have hit me between the eyes."

"ENOUGH!" Kirby threw Peg's hairbrush across the room. It hit the armoire and clattered to the floor. Unperturbed, the Confederate soldier turned to look out the window again.

"Do I have to call the innkeeper?"

"It wouldn't make any difference."

The man's equanimity puzzled Kirby. Did the innkeeper hire this wacko to keep an eye on him until they found Peg? Was he hurt worse than he thought? "What's your name?"

"Private Jack Daily. Seventh Louisiana Infantry. Hays' Brigade."

More Civil War nonsense. "Mr. Daily, I'm not feeling well. I'd like you to leave now." Kirby marched across the room. Reaching for Jack's elbow to escort him to the door, he gasped as his hand went through the soldier's arm. Kirby drew back and rubbed his chilled fingers. "What are you," he whispered.

"You HAD to do that, didn't you?" Jack brushed invisible wrinkles from his sleeve. "I was standing here not bothering anyone and you get all worked up and go after me."

"What do you want of me?" Kirby could hardly get the words out.

"I don't want anything. I was here first."

Kirby had never heard of any ghosts at The Brafferton, but old places like this soaked up sorrowful experiences like a bloody sponge. Did the inn have painful memories too? "Why do I see you?"

Jack returned his gaze to the accident scene. "I don't know exactly. Most folks don't."

Already losing his fear, Kirby peeked out the window too. Emergency vehicles and firemen filled the intersection. They were lifting the woman's body out of the wreckage. "Why her? If the light had changed ten seconds sooner she'd be safe now."

"I don't rightly know." Jack stood at attention while the attendants arranged the body on a gurney and covered it with a sheet.

"It's so arbitrary." Kirby swallowed back tears.

"Aye."

The trucker who'd caused the accident hovered near the wreckage, wringing his hands. "Look at that poor bastard." Kirby wiped the corner of his eye with his knuckle. "One stupid mistake and he kills someone."

"Welcome to hell, brother," Jack said through clenched teeth.

Kirby focused on the gurney sliding into the back of the ambulance and touched the bottle of Valium in his pocket. "You made the trip to the other side?"

"Aye."

"You know how things are?"

Jack shrugged. "I know about how. I'm short on why."

A sudden thought struck Kirby. "I'm not dead am I?"

Jack snorted. "Do you feel dead?"

Kirby touched the glass over the air conditioner, leaving a fingerprint. Disappointed, he frowned. "No."

"Don't rush it, my friend. It doesn't solve anything."

"I just want peace."

The ghost laughed again. "What do you expect? Cherubs and harps? Paradise? You are still yourself on this side of the veil."

"Then what's the point?" Kirby had counted on things being okay once he passed on. No more guilt. No more sorrow. No more nightmares. A clean slate.

"There is no point." Jack took off his hat and held it over his heart. The trucker stood in the middle of York Street watching the ambulance bearing the young woman's body drive away. "You move on. It's as simple as that."

The room was icy cold. Kirby hugged himself, trying not to think about the crushing burden of culpability that never went away no matter how sorry you were.

A policeman took the trucker's arm and led him to a squad car parked in front of the church.

"What are you looking for, my friend?" Jack fixed Kirby through the corner of his eye. "Absolution?"

Kirby was taken aback. "I'd hoped -- that's what they preach anyway."

"Doesn't that strike you as immoral? Shuffling off your debts onto some other innocent soul?"

Kirby had to admit he thought the preacher's version of redemption seemed too easy. "I guess I was being unrealistic."

Jack returned his gaze to the accident scene. "You have a bad case of soldier's heart."

Such quaint terms for the devastation of war -- soldier's heart, shell shock, battle fatigue. It went on and on -- generation after generation. How could the doctor think that the suffering of others would somehow ease Kirby's personal nightmare?

Jack craned his neck. The trucker was trying to explain -- pointing down York Street, then at the wreckage in the intersection. "We'd be monsters if what we did didn't bother us."

Kirby leaned his forehead against the window. "Maybe we are monsters for doing what we did in the first place."

"I was a boy when I went to war." Jack shifted his musket to the other shoulder and moved so he could view the street from another angle. "My brother and I were going to be heroes. We were fighting against tyranny and for freedom. People would look up to us and thank us for our service. It seemed right and moral at the time."

The policeman took a notepad out of his pocket -- scribbled something -- asked a question. The trucker slumped his shoulders and shook his head.

Kirby understood the trucker's instinct to deny responsibility. It was natural. A moment of carelessness -- or irrational fear -- or anger could have such awful consequences. He squeezed his eyes shut. "I volunteered for the Marines in 1944 with my best friends -- Jimmy O'Rourke and Billy Benson. I was engaged to Billy's little sister at the time. There was a party at the firehouse to send us off. I felt ten feet tall. It was the last time I can remember being truly happy with myself."

Jack turned away from the window and backed into the corner. "I didn't think about dying. That was something that happened to other guys. I thought about killing though." He sighed. "I was a fool."

The policeman slipped the notebook into his back pocket and pointed to the squad car. The trucker turned around and put his hands on the roof of the cruiser. The cop patted his sides, feeling his pockets. Handcuffing the man's hands behind him, he put him in the vehicle and drove away. Another policeman set out yellow traffic cones and began directing cars around the accident site.

"The Japs attacked us. We were going to kick their butts all the way back across the Pacific Ocean." The movie in Kirby's head sped up -- the mad race across the beach and up the slope in knee deep sand, the massive explosion that threw him on his back, the bits of brain and bone that clung to his body. Memories he'd avoided for over sixty years washed over him. Oblivion was better. He reached for the pills in his pocket.

Jack bowed his head. "When I left my post that day, I was running away. I came here -- to this room -- to die."

Shocked by Jack's words, Kirby fumbled the medicine bottle. The cap came off and yellow pills rolled across the rug. How many old soldiers found their way to The Brafferton, he wondered. How many troubled souls had taken refuge in this room?

"Gettysburg was chaotic. The wounded from both sides lay moaning in the streets. My brother and I chased a "Bluecoat" through the Diamond. Near High Street a cannonball blew Daniel's leg off. He bled to death in minutes crying for our mother. As he paled and left me in a pool of gore, I saw the Federal we'd been chasing head back toward York. I lost my head and went after the bastard." Jack voice trembled. "Just as he reached that intersection right out there, I sent the bastard to hell with a musket ball through the head."

A tow truck arrived to retrieve what was left of the yellow Honda. "Justice," Kirby muttered as he watched a second one drive away with the wrecked truck. "Did that make you feel better?"

"Aye. At first it felt damn good. I ran up and kicked the son of a bitch in the ribs. That's for my baby brother, I yelled. That's for Daniel. My shot destroyed most of the face, but I knew he was young because he had no facial hair whatever -- not even peach fuzz. I stripped off his tunic looking for ammunition. It was then I saw that this wasn't a boy but a woman. She'd stuffed a pistol in the front of her trousers. When I removed it, I was shocked to realize that she was with child. I backed away. There were people in the church taking care of the wounded but I couldn't face them -- or anyone. I turned toward the Diamond. Bleeding soldiers limped my way leaning on their muskets. Dazed, I ducked into the butcher shop and then into this house."

"You'd just lost your brother. She was dressed like the enemy -- how were you to know?"

"It was quiet up here. The toys made me think of Daniel when we were boys. I remembered the fear in my mother's eyes when we left home. She told us to take care of each other. The numbness gave way to pain. I couldn't go home without my brother. I'd rather lie down on the bed with the woman's pistol under my chin than tell our mother Daniel was dead."

"One quick pull on the trigger," Kirby said dreamily.

"I lay there thinking about Daniel and the girl and her baby and the Minié ball that just missed me. The bed was soft and a warm breeze came in through the broken window. I heard voices in the street. After awhile, my arm got tired and I let the pistol drop onto the bed. I remembered the scrap of ham in my pocket and stuffed it in my mouth. As I chewed, I looked around the room. After a bit I got up and went back out into the street."

"What made you stop?"

"The ham was greasy."

"Greasy?"

194

"And my canteen was empty."

"You didn't kill yourself because you were thirsty?"

"No. I didn't kill myself because when I went to find water, I saw her body lying in the street."

A loud screech from the street startled Kirby. The workers hooked the crumpled yellow car to the tow truck and pulled it away from the post.

Kirby's breathing escalated -- short quick inhalations as the flashback swept over him. There was no escaping the smell. It clung to him like sticky black molasses. Big black beetles crawled over the corpses. Kirby flicked one off Jimmy O'Rourke's stiff hand. Scuffling footsteps in the distance. Kirby cowered behind the pile of bodies until he couldn't stand it anymore. Jumping to his feet, he fired into the darkness until there were no more bullets in his rifle. "Die, you yellow bastard," he shouted before dropping behind the rotting remains of his friends.

"I couldn't leave her there," Jack continued. "And I had to go take care of Daniel."

At dawn, Kirby peeked over the pile of bodies. Something yellow fluttered in the distance. Kirby looked left and right before crawling out to investigate.

"I carried the girl to the church over there although I knew she was dead." Jack pointed out the window. "I figured someone would take care of her eventually."

Kirby sucked in air faster and faster.

"Then I went looking for Daniel. I ran back to where his blood stained High Street. He was gone. I raced through Gettysburg -- checking the houses and barns and stables and stores -- turning over bodies lying on the streets and on stretchers outside the hospitals."

Kirby slithered across the rocky ground on his belly zeroing in on the flash of color. As he got closer, he saw a dead Marine lying on his side. The man had tied a yellow scarf around his bloody arm. SHIT! SHIT! SHIT! Kirby pounded the earth with his fists. He'd killed another American.

"I wandered throughout the town looking for Daniel all night and most of the next day. In the afternoon, the guns started again. I knew I should go back to my unit but I couldn't until I found Daniel. I came back and hid in this room -- standing guard at this window, watching that church in case someone brought in my brother's body."

Kirby rolled the Marine over. His eyes bulged. It was Billy Benson. Peg's big brother -- his last remaining friend from home. He must have screamed but he couldn't remember hearing it. "I'm sorry, I'm sorry!" The tourniquet was too loose. Maybe if he tightened it, Billy would have a chance. Sure. That's all he needed. Then he'd be fine. He retied the yellow scarf on the dead boy's arm. There now. That's better. Sliding his hands under Billy's armpits, he pulled him back toward the wall of corpses. "Let's get out of here before a sniper sees us." He was halfway across the clearing when he saw the gut wound.

"I hid here on the third day too. The war went on without me. I went home to face mother's sorrow -- and my own. I lived another seventy years looking for Daniel." The ghost turned back toward the church. "I'm still looking for him."

"They pinned us down, you see -- and they all died -- everyone but me." It was impossible for anyone who wasn't there to understand. That knowledge had kept Kirby mute since 1945. How could he tell Peg about Billy? How could he tell anyone?

A road worker swept up the glittering pieces of glass in the road below them. "They are clearing away the last of the wreckage," Jack reported.

Kirby sighed. So now he knew why he felt rotten -- why he had nightmares, why loud noises made him flinch. What good was that? It didn't change things. Billy wasn't coming back -- nor Jimmy O'Rourke or Daniel Daily or the pregnant woman Jack killed or the girl in the yellow Honda.

"Here comes the innkeeper with your wife," Jack said softly.

"I better get these pills back into Peg's bag."

The front door opened. "He's upstairs." Kirby heard the innkeeper say.

"I'm coming, Kirby darling." Peg sounded out of breath.

Kirby stuffed the pill bottle under the cushion and sat down in the high backed chair, bracing himself to face Peg. "Are you still there?" He whispered over his shoulder to the ghost.

"Aye. We all are."

Historical Notes

By Mindy Phillips Lawrence

1935 Labor Day Hurricane -- Islamorada, Florida

Islamorada is a cluster of islands in the Florida Keys. It includes Plantation, Windley, Upper Matecumbe, Lower Matecumbe, Liunmvitae and Indian Keys. The area attracted sailors, Indians and other settlers because of the freshwater wells located on Lower Matecumbe. When an entrepreneur built a railway through the keys in the 1850s, the area flourished.

In late August of 1935, a tropical disturbance formed off Africa and headed across the Atlantic toward Cuba and Florida. Six hundred and fifty World War I veterans were camped on Matecumbe Key. Because of Franklin Roosevelt's New Deal, these men were building US Highway One that was to link Miami and Key West. By mid-day September 2nd, the weather was so bad that federal officials dispatched a train from Miami to evacuate the workers. About twenty miles north of Islamorada, the locomotive stopped to pick up passengers. When it did, a loose cable snapped delaying it for more than an hour. When the train pulled into the station around eight P.M., the hurricane hit. As the workers struggled to climb aboard, an eighteen-foot tidal surge swept over the island washing the railway cars from the track and tipping them over on their sides. Houses buckled under the tremendous pressure. People were blown into the sea, killed by flying debris or crushed under the train. Witnesses reported flashing lights -- static electricity generated by sand lifted into the air by the roaring wind.

The hurricane became the worst storm ever recorded with winds gusting up to two hundred, fifty miles an hour.

When it was over, all but one of Matecumbe's buildings were gone. A two-story house floated in Florida Bay minus its roof. Trees were broken off just above the ground. Bodies rendered faceless by flying sand and water littered the area. Although no one knows exactly how many people were lost, the coroner's report listed four hundred, twenty-three known deaths. Many people simply vanished. Unidentified skeletons washed up on islands in the bay for years.

Kristallnacht, The Night of Broken Glass

On October 28, 1938, the Nazis arrested all Jews living in Germany but bearing Polish citizenship and sent them across the border into Poland. When the Polish government refused to admit them, the Germans interned the seventeen thousand Jews in "relocation camps" along the Polish frontier. One of these deportees was Zindel Grynszpan, born in western Poland but a resident of Hanover since 1911. On the night of October 27th, German police forced Grynszpan and his family out of their home.

Herschel Grynszpan, Zindel's seventeen-year-old son, received news of his family's expulsion in Paris where he was living with an uncle. On November 7, he went to the German embassy to assassinate the ambassador. When he discovered that his target was not there, he shot Third Secretary Ernst von Rath who died two days later.

Joseph Goebbels, Hitler's Chief of Propaganda, called Grynszpan's attack a conspiracy by "International Jewry" against the Reich and the Fuhrer. Goebbels used this assassination as the catalyst for a pogrom against the Jews.

On November 9th and 10th, gangs of Germans, Austrians and people from the Sudetenland attacked Jews in the streets and in their homes, businesses and synagogues. They also desecrated cemeteries and vandalized schools. At least ninety-six Jews died with hundreds more injured. The Nazis arrested thirty thousand Jews and sent them to concentration camps.

Three days later on November 12th, Goebbels, Hermann Goering, Reinhard Heydrich, Walter Funk and other Nazi officials met to assess the damage done at *Kristallnacht*. They made the victims responsible for the destruction and laid down laws that prevented further Jewish participation in the German economy.

The Story of Sugihara

In 1939, the Japanese government sent Chiune Sugihara and his wife to Kaunas, Lithuania to open a consulate service. Chiune had barely arrived when Hitler's armies sent a flood of Jewish refugees into Lithuania from Poland. The new arrivals had no money and no possessions, no place to go and no place to stay. Although the local Jewish population tried to help, the situation was overwhelming. The refugees had only one way out – through the Soviet Union to Japan.

Then the Soviets invaded Lithuania on June 15, 1940 trapping the refugees. However, for the time being, Soviet authorities allowed Jews to migrate across the Soviet Union as long as they could obtain the papers to do so. This of course was almost impossible since few governments would issue them the correct visas.

The refugees did have sympathetic resources in the area. When the Soviets instructed all foreign embassies to leave

Kaunas in June 1940, Chine Sugihara requested and received a twenty-day extension. Learning that the Dutch colonial islands of Curacao and Dutch Guiana (Suriname) did not require formal entry papers, Chiune worked with acting Dutch consul, Jan Zwartendijk, to get as many passports and entry permits stamped as possible. The idea was to send the Jews to Japan, then on to other places.

A problem arose. When a flood of Polish Jews arrived in late July 1940, Sugihara knew he could not help them without permission from the Japanese Foreign Ministry in Tokyo. Three times he sent a message to them and was denied. Brought up in the strict Samurai tradition of obedience, Sugihara believed he should help those in need. Risking his life and career, he defied his own government and signed the visas thus saving many Jewish lives.

Cleveland Circus Fire of 1942

It was August 4, 1942, the second of a four-day, eight-show tour for Ringling Brothers Circus in Cleveland, Ohio. The north side of Lakeside at East 9th street buzzed with activity as the performers readied themselves for the next performance.

At 11:45 A.M., a pile of straw at the west end of the menagerie ignited. Flames shot up the paraffin and benzene-coated tent walls in seconds. Two companies of Cleveland firefighters arrived with a high-pressure hose unit. In spite of their attempts, it took only fifteen minutes for the menagerie to burn to the ground, killing many of the animals and burning others. Two human injuries were recorded -- the elephant trainer who was burned trying to save the animals from death and another employee who was hit by an elephant hook.

No one ever discovered the cause of the fire. The property sustained $200,000 in damages, not covered by insurance.

The show went on that night without the many animals that had died. Circus owner John Ringling North, said, "I can stand the loss incurred in the fire, but I just cannot stand to see the animals suffer."

Rosie the Riveter

During World War II, every able-bodied man gave up his civilian job and joined the military. Industry struggled to find enough workers to make goods for the war effort.

The government launched a media campaign to convince American women to enter the workforce in factories, lumber and steel mills and transportation. Print, film and radio encouraged women to take over men's jobs using a mythical character named Rosie the Riveter. Designed by J. Howard Miller, Rosie wore a red bandanna covering her hair and had a rolled back sleeve on her blue bib overalls exposing a flexed female bicep. The bold over-sized caption on the posters read, "We Can Do It!"

The advertising campaign encouraged women to "Do the job he left behind." Although Rosie urged women to leave their secretarial positions, domestic jobs and low-salary industrial work, it taught women that they could be successful in men's positions, even if the time was not ripe for women to stay in those fields when the war was over.

Camp Tarawa

The population of Kamuela (Waimea) in December 1942 was around four hundred. Two weeks into 1943, the population exploded to twenty-five thousand. Most of the influx of people was a contingent of U.S. Marines, survivors of the Battle of Tarawa in the Gilbert Islands. They came by the truckload and established an enormous tent city.

The owners of the sprawling Parker Ranch leased forty thousand acres to the U.S. Government for $1 per year. The military turned it into the largest Marine Corps training site in the Pacific. More that fifty thousand soldiers passed through its gates before the end of World War II. An area located between the snow-capped mountains of Mauna Kea and Mauna Loa became Camp Tarawa. Many young men recovered from battle there but it was more than a recreation spot for wounded or exhausted soldiers. It was a classified facility where troops trained for top-secret missions.

The first group of Marines - the Second Division - arrived in December 1943, back from the assault on Betio Island, Tarawa Atoll. They came to heal and train for an upcoming mission. The second group, The 27th Marine Regiment, formed at Camp Pendleton, California, relocated to Camp Tarawa, Hawaii in August 1944 as part of the Fifth Division. There, they trained along with the others for their first combat assignment -- The Battle of Iwo Jima.

The Battle of Iwo Jima

For ten weeks in early 1945, the United States Navy executed the longest sustained aerial offensive of World War II against an isolated island in the south Pacific known as Iwo Jima. The goal was to damage the Japanese ability to fight before American troops landed on the beach. However, the bombardment had little effect on the twenty-one thousand Japanese troops burrowed in the volcanic rock, touching few of their underground fortresses.

On February 19th, approximately seventy thousand troops on 880 ships prepared to hit the beaches. The island was important to support B-29 raids on mainland Japan. The US also wanted to prevent Japanese kamikaze pilots from using the island's three airstrips. At 8:59 A.M., the United States Marines headed toward shore. Unfortunately, military strategists underestimated Japanese strength by as much as seventy percent. Also, the nature and difficulty of the soil on the island was never contemplated in the planning stages of the battle. The carnage on the beaches below Suribachi was horrific as wave after wave of Marines landed and fought their way inland.

On February 20th, the Marines started their advance toward Mount Suribachi. Japanese entrenched in the mountain had to be incinerated with flamethrowers. The troops had close air support by Naval and Marine pilots, sometimes only a few hundred yards from the Marines.

On February 23th, a photographer took the famous photo of the American flag being raised on the summit of Suribachi. However, it wasn't until March 25th that the last pockets of Japanese resistance were secured at Kitano Point.

The Marines sustained 23,573 casualties with 19,117 of those killed in action. Over a third of the Marines who participated in the invasion were killed, wounded or suffered from extreme battle fatigue.

The Kent State Shootings

On May 2, 1970, the governor of Ohio sent National Guard troops to Kent State University to suppress student protests of President Nixon's policies in Vietnam and Cambodia. Mid-day on May 4th, guardsmen threw tear gas canisters and advanced on a group of students with fixed bayonets. When some protesters threw rocks at the troops, guardsmen fired on the crowd without warning -- sixty-seven shots in thirteen seconds. When the shooting stopped, four Kent State students lay dead with nine wounded. The four students killed at Kent State were Allison Krause, Sandra Lee Scheuer, Jeffrey Miller and William K. Schroeder. The closest casualty was at least twenty yards away from the troops. The farthest was two hundred, fifty yards away.

The Brafferton in Gettysburg

Samuel Gettys purchased a land grant of over three hundred acres in Pennsylvania in the 1760's. His family moved to the area and built roads, houses and a tavern. When Samuel declared bankruptcy, his son James Getty bought one hundred, sixteen acres that included the tavern.

Michael Hoke, a tanner who worked with the Gettys family, purchased a lot from Gettys in 1786 and built a brownstone on it. In 1843, the owner sold the house and land to Nicholas Cordori for $1600. He bought additional land on both sides of the house, expanded it for his family of eleven children and added his meat market to the east side. It was here where the Cordoni's hid in the basement on July first, second and third of 1863 as shots flew in the Battle of Gettysburg. A Minié ball from the first day of battle still graces the mantle in one of the rooms. The house acted as a Catholic hospital after the battle was over.

After living there for one hundred, twenty-four years, the Cordoni's sold the property to Jim and Mini Agard in 1986. They named it the Brafferton after Brafferton Hall at the College of William and Mary in Williamsburg. The Agards opened the house as the second bed and breakfast in Gettysburg. Since 1993, the Brafferton has changed hands several times but it remains a intrinsic part of historical Gettysburg.

Bibliography

Armitage, Michael. *World War II Day by Day*. New York: DK, 2004.

Bellamy, John S. *The Corpse in the Cellar & Other Tales of Cleveland Woe: Incredible But True Stories of Cleveland Crime and Disaster*. Cleveland: Gray, 1999.

Bradley, James. *Flags of Our Fathers: Heroes of Iwo Jima*. New York: Bantam, 2000.

Caputo, Philip. *A Rumor of War*. New York: Holt, 1996.

Colman, Penny. *Rosie the Riveter: Women Working on the Home Front in World War II*. New York: Crown, 1995.

Drye, Willie. *Storm of the Century: The Labor Day Hurricane of 1935*. N.p.: National Geographic, 2003.

Gluck, Sherna. *Rosie the Riveter Revisited: Women, the War, and Social Change*. N.p.: New American Library, 1988.

Gordon, William A. *Four Dead in Ohio: Was There a Conspiracy at Kent State*. [Lake Forest]: North Ridge, 1995.

Grossman, David A. *On Killing : The Psychological Cost of Learning to Kill in War and Society*. N.p.: Grossman, 1996.

Michener, James A. *Kent State: What Happened and Why*. New York: Random, 1982.

Ross, Bill D. *Iwo Jima : Legacy of Valor*. N.p.: Random, 1986.

Wright, Derrick. *Battle for Iwo Jima, 1945*. Phoenix, GB: Sutton, 1999.

More Great Books from Red Engine Press

Losing Patience by Joyce Faulkner
ISBN: 978-0-9745652-4-5 $15.95

These tales remind one of classic episodes of the *Twilight Zone.*

They Came Home: Korean War POWs Tell Their Stories
by Pat McGrath Avery
ISBN: 978-0-9743758-6-1 $14.95

True stories of three soldiers who were prisoners of war in Korea.

Caribbean Calling by J. D. Gordon
ISBN: 978-0-9745652-1-0 $14.95

Adventure, action and romance unfolding in the Caribbean.

Have Poem Will Travel by S. Dale "Sierra" Seawright
ISBN: 978-0-9745652-3-7 $9.95

Reminiscent of the rhythms of Loretta Lynn, Woody Guthrie and Pete Seeger.

One Blue Star by Mindy Phillips Lawrence
ISBN: 978-0-9745652-5-3 $9.95

The lunacy and sorrow of war from the point of view of a parent waiting for her boy to come home.

The Aged Tree Stands Proud by Pat McGrath Avery
ISBN: 978-0-9663276-1-6 $10.95

An emotional journey through life.

Children's Titles from Red Engine Press

Miller the Green Caterpillar by Darrell House
Illustrated by Patti Argoff
ISBN: 978-0-9663276-9-1 $16.95

A tale of determination, vision and the belief that sometimes wishes do come true. Ages 3 – 8.

Underneath the Cushions On The Couch
by Darrell House $15.95

This CD of children's songs appeal to the kid in all of us. The rollicking title song makes us laugh at the obvious. All ages.

The Path Winds Home by Janie DeVos
Illustrated by Nancy Marsh
ISBN: 978-0-9743758-0-2 $16.95

A must read for a child in today's diversified and multicultural society. The book is in hardcover. Ages 2 – 8.

How High Can You Fly? by Janie DeVos
Illustrated by Renee Rejent
ISBN: 978-0-9663276-2-4 $16.95

A story about self-esteem and acceptance of others. Ages 2 – 8.

Tommy's War by Pat McGrath Avery
Illustrated by Eric Ray
ISBN: 978-0-9663276-8-3 $5.95

Tommy and his friend each have a parent that leaves home because of a war. Ages 4 – 7.

These book are available from your local bookstore, on-line supplier or Red Engine Press (www.redenginepress.com).

About the Author

Joyce Faulkner is a freelance writer living in Pittsburgh, Pennsylvania. She studied writing at the University of Arkansas and holds a degree in Chemical Engineering from the University of Pittsburgh and an MBA from Cleveland State. Her professional interests include Knowledge Management, Business Process Engineering, eCommerce and Internet Marketing. Her private passions include aviation, history, travel and philosophy. *In the Shadow of Suribachi* is her second book. She is at work on several novels.